For my grandmother who, at an early age, was the first person to show me the magic.

These journeys took place many years ago. In a time and place much different than today. In those days the internet was barely accessible to travelers. Internet cafes and pay phones were the best way to contact home, or God forbid, a handwritten letter. It was a time of chaos and triumph and maybe even a little insanity. When, for a brief moment, I was able to lift the mantle of attachment and travel unhindered through the universe.

In the beginning there was only the rain and the cold September afternoon, the windshield wipers going WOMP WOMP and the smell of burnt oil and confusion that hung on like biscuits and gravy..

There was a road....

The check engine light came on as we struggled up the steepest hill in the whole damn Pacific coast range and before we knew it a loud POP!!!! KNOCK!! KNOCK!! KNOCK!! In the engine. The sound, like some demonic mechanic bang!! BANGING!!! His way out of a combustible tomb.

Pulling off the road outside a small coastal town surrounded by redwoods and tall pines. Ahead of us is the gray. The deep gray two laned highway that wound its way as unforgiving as the last three hundred. In the distance on either side lay small dairy farms that quietly sat in ignorance as our hearts filled with the sad knowledge that we were broke, and now with a broken vehicle.

"What should we do now" was the simple question asked by the lady.

"The only thing we can do" I say quietly.

There was a needed moment to think. To let the fog and spider webs run from the jagged space in my brain. The car was done. The engine continued to tick and moan as smokey tendrils drifted out of its belly.

Further investigation, outside in the damn cold rain, there under the hood, was an angry gash where a rod had been thrown through the engine wall.

Back again in the warmth of the car she looks at me and asks.

"What should we leave behind?" In that quiet voice of hers.

This is real life, I think. To be stranded desperately without a soul around on a lonely aching coast.

"Ok so let's grab what we can carry and ditch the rest"! I said, snapping out of a cold haze.

Looking around at the human clutter of board games and cooking gear; a stove and pots and pans. Blankets and pillows, towels and tents, the list goes on and on.....

In the way that these things usually go, mild hysteria came in with the afternoon tide, as the panic to choose wisely weighed us down. There was a distinct understanding that when we were rid of the car we would be alone with the road and half our gear.

Coastal California never quite freezes but the wind and rain and general sogginess make for a harsh environment when you don't have a roof over your head.

It was that way when we stood almost naked on the side of the road like beggars. Or bugs. Bugs spattered against the windshield of some rich asshole in a warm and sleek Mercedes Benz.

A ride in this weather was almost a miracle, and when an old red truck pulled over for us it was just that, a miracle. The guy was some stoned hippy that immediately lit up a huge joint and said "ASS, grass, or cash take your pick mother fucker!"

I knew this would be an interesting experience as we coasted down the highway like buccaneers. Drinking hi-octane booze straight from the can and listening to devilish hillbilly rock and roll. The man's nostrils flared like an old steamboat and there were lines of insanity all over his mouth. Sara had to adjust in the back seat when she realized that she was sitting on some monstrosity that later turned out to be a cat. An old scoundrel named Threadbare. His claws were still sharp even if his brain had turned to mush when his owner ran him over three years ago. The cat had healed himself, he muttered as smoke poured from his varicose face. It seemed to be coming from everywhere. Through his nose and even through the coarse hairs on his balding head. Each hair spouting fumes like small chemical factories.

Eight months and twenty-three seconds later, or so it seemed... Really it was only about three and a half minutes and then there it was like an oasis. The off ramp for the next town over.

"Yeah bro, that's a great story! Here's just grand, yep, right there that's perfect!"

Then we're piling out like tarantulas in a banana heap. Groping for our cluttered things. It's still raining and there are little rivulets and waterways trying to grab our gear. And I'm saying to that crazy bastard through the cracked window to get lost or I'll shove my foot up his ass....

After that it's all elbows and knees after he takes off screaming like a battered road demon. Were on the side of the road with our things scattered and our dreams shattered.

Nothing else to do but keep going. So two more outstretched thumbs and about twenty two minutes later a little happy sedan with a cheery old mop of a woman screams to a halt and with warmth like a June bug says...

"Jump in kids, it's cold outside........."

Chapter 1

The Beginning

When Hernan Cortez, the Spanish explorer turned murderer, sent a contingency of men north from Mexico, he expected to find the route to India. His men on the other hand expected to find the lost kingdom of Queen Calafia. The dark skinned warrior woman that ruled over an army of beautiful bare breasted Amazons.

So when the half starved conquistadors arrived in the land that would come to be known as California, they fully expected a regal scene. Instead they were met with scurvy and savage warriors who seemed to know straight away that these new people did not belong.

It felt that way, as Autumn came to a close and our situation had not improved. In the three weeks after the car had gone up in flames we had struggled our way down the coast with nothing but the gear we brought from the smoking husk of our exploded car. We've moved through every run-down logging town from Crescent City to Eureka looking for work, or a warm bed to spend the night.

After being chased out of a makeshift campsite by a local police officer and forced back onto the unforgiving highway, we've found ourselves again with our thumbs extended.

Hitchhiking is an art. And unfortunately the only art worth a damn is the kind that makes you suffer. It's a gradual suffering. At first you're excited. Nervous with anticipation and full of energy for the adventure. But that doesn't last. After the first hour you start to lose patience. Then time seems to stop working and everything moves in slow motion as the cars pass, flying by at nine million miles an hour, as if to say, no thanks bub, I don't feel like getting murdered today. So we switch sides and now Sara is in front with her million dollar smile and her leg extended suggestively.

There is a misconception that California is a carefree land of happy go lucky hippies. They do exist, they are just rare, usually living in vans down by the river in magical little communities that are hard to find. The majority of Californians are indifferent, exhausted locals with major trust issues regarding the wandering folk, street people and gutter punks. These folks are just plum tired of the bums who filter in and out of the small towns along the coast. Hoping for handouts or a place to lay their drug addled heads. Mostly on benches and behind buildings but also sometimes right in front of schools and on the lawns of distinguished community members' homes. "This will not do", says Sally Jones on the committee for community excellence. So the fuzz has been notified and every man with a badge knows to give the boot to any of the wayfaring souls.

"I'm so sick of this. That cop was an asshole" Sara says, as we reach the grass patch next to the onramp of Highway 101 at the south end of the Eureka city limits.

"What was he supposed to do? We were camping in the city park. At least he didn't give us a ticket." I say, huffing and puffing after carrying the tent and sleeping bags through the thick brush of the forest.

"I can't believe you're defending that dick. He called you a smelly hippy." She says, half angry but with a smile on her face.

"Well, maybe I am a smelly hippy. I haven't showered in like ten days. I'm sick of this shit too. We need to find something soon or just give up and go home." I say, defeated and with the gloom of the early afternoon, a little down in my soul.

"How would we even do that?"

"We could call our parents."

"No way. I am not doing that. The look on their faces, can you imagine?" She says angrily.

"It's getting cold and we're on our last few dollars. I have that final paycheck coming but not soon enough. We need to do something." I say with my thumbs desperately outstretched as a train of cars sweep past us sending gusts of wind and small waves of dirty water to splatter over our things. In the last two weeks we had slept in the private bathroom at a roadside hotel's pool, leaving early enough in the morning to avoid being caught by the front desk. But also under a highway underpass, tucked way up into the crevice where the earth almost touches the concrete. And then sometimes we'd get lucky like the last few nights in Eureka, popping our tent up just off a nearby trail in a giant redwood grove. Our tiny shelter, dwarfed by the goliath trees but still in sight of angry locals who feared that we were the monsters in the night.

"Ooo look, that van is slowing down and pulling over!" Sara shouts as we grab our things and awkwardly run to the waiting vehicle. It's an old blue van that has soccer mom written all over it. The sliding door opens electronically as we approach and a friendly head peeks out from the driver's seat. Her name is Carol and she can take us as far as Leggett. And so it goes for the rest of the afternoon. After Carol it was a sporty little red car with an over-caffeinated, but friendly real estate agent who remembers hitchhiking when it was safe back in the late eighties. And then it's another and another as we slowly crawl south towards the bay.

We had just been dropped off by a friendly hippy who after about a hundred miles of winding mountain roads and several hours of good conversation deposited a handful of weed and a twenty-dollar bill in our hands. It was for the "munchies" he had said. With a smile and wave he pulled away and we found ourselves alone in the small coastal county of Mendocino.

Mendocino is a special place, removed from the rest of California by impenetrable mountains and winding roads that frequently are the subject of floods, landslides and forest fires. From just about any direction it will take the traveler hours to navigate the back roads. If you are coming from Highway 101 in the interior of the state you'll have some of the steepest and most treacherous roads in the country waiting for you.

But it is not without its rewards. For those that attempt the journey they are sure to be met with jaw dropping scenery the entire way. Coming out of the mountains the traveler arrives in Anderson Valley. First settled by European farmers in the mid eighteen hundreds, the land eventually developed its own language, Bootling, an amalgamation of English, Gaelic and Spanish. The locals love to tell of the early speakers of the language and a few people like to pretend that they can speak it…

The capital of this narrow valley that runs its way along the Navarro river all the way to the great Pacific ocean is Boonville and its inhabitants are now mostly rogues, vintners, artists and pot farmers. In the late summer the hills take on a golden fleece that runs all the way to the top where the mighty California oak, spruce and redwood form an emerald green crown. Winding through the valley you pass all of the finest, secret wineries that have not yet made international headlines and with it the hordes of wealthy tourists. Past the valley and the road will eventually lead you through one of the last great redwood forests before you hit San Francisco and Muir woods. Here you can find some of the tallest trees in the world. Past all of this and finally, after many long winding stretches of road you will find yourself face to face with an almost empty stretch of coastline. Dramatic, vicious, mysterious. Miles of rugged cliffs that plummet down into mermaid green waters.

The village that we've been dropped off in is nestled away in a lovely little bay surrounded by tall pines and the occasional redwood. Our driver had told us of a perfect place to make a secret camp just north of the town near a beach with giant windswept dunes. The megalithic sand piles were covered in breezy grass with scattered driftwood and sea bird nests. The dunes would provide shelter from the biting wind and block the road from uninvited guests.

Those "uninvited guests" usually ended up being wired meth heads out for a wander. Taking a break from our travels we stopped, rolled a generous joint from the handful of crumpled rolling papers and puffed away. The sea in front of us had transformed into a raging maelstrom with white caps and sea spray. It was difficult lighting our smoke and after several curses, cupped hands and about thirty matches we settled into a conclave amongst the massive dunes and watched the ocean, wondering what would come next.

"This place should be perfect for a couple nights. We can put the tent up when it gets dark and maybe even have a fire with some of the driftwood." I say, excited and allowing myself to relax with the good weed.

"I want a fire now, it's chilly." She says, rubbing her arms to warm herself and leaning in close to me for the body heat.

"We don't want to attract attention. It will be dark soon."

With the strong weed and our energy completely spent from the long day of hitchhiking we relaxed into the sand and contemplated our existence. Just a few weeks before we had been average everyday people. Going to work in our average, ordinary office jobs in the busy capital of New York. Plugging into the machine day after day and feeding the beast of corporate America. Long months of this had started to deteriorate our souls. We could feel ourselves slipping into the abyss of mediocrity.

And now, weeks later, we are here. On this lonely beach, watching the waves and the seabirds with twenty dollars to our name. Instead of a suit I wore tattered jeans and an oil stained fisherman's sweater. Sara, instead of business casual and a name tag, wore a hooded poncho and corduroy bell bottoms that already had a tear in the knee.

After some time, the sun started to slip beneath the angry waves and it was time to get up to shake off the sand and start our evening routine. Scattered driftwood, dried out from the wind and the sun were collected and put into a pile in an indent in the dunes. The wind would be less aggressive here and perfect for a fire and campsite. The area surrounding our little beach was thick with massive trees and deep fern forests. Exploring a bit of the beach we discovered a small river emptying into a tiny lagoon. There were rocky cliffs that towered overhead that made it easier to hide the tent, which was quickly set up and snuggled into the dunes. Soon afterwards a healthy fire was started. The tinder and the dried driftwood were lit easily and we stretched our fingers over the crackly fire to warm our soggy joints.

"That feels so nice." Sara says while snuggling into the warmth of the fire and the soft sand underneath. "This is the perfect spot" She says while glancing around the camp. The clouds had cleared to reveal a thousand twinkling stars and the smell of the smoking driftwood began to make my stomach growl.

"I'm hungry. We should break out the last of the food. Let's celebrate." I say, excited for our new found comforts.

The meal that night was meager, a loaf of bread, a hunk of cheese and an over ripe tomato, along with a cheap bottle of wine. We happily laid out the food on a blanket and began to prepare the meal. Looking back at our beautiful sandwiches it would have been a pathetic meal to anyone other than us, but at the time it seemed like a feast. One of those old-fashioned kinds, where you slaughter a goat and throw the whole thing on the grill, hooves and all. We tipped the bottle and passed the joint and all seemed well in our temporary paradise by the sea.

We sang songs and told stories. I recited from my tattered copy of *The Prophet* and took long swigs of wine. We were transformed from the jobless vagrants that we were, to the great explorers of our imagination! In those few hours before the fire died out we reached past the confusion of the last few weeks to a special place full of magic. It's hard to explain in words, but there's a feeling you get when you know you have nothing else to lose. When you reach the bottom and it's as pleasant as a warm fire and the angry freezing sea, then what else can you do? You either enjoy the moment or you go stark raving mad. There is something really special about being really truly hungry. The kind of hunger that gnaws at your insides, tearing away your spirit by the hour. The first bite of this pathetic meal was as delicious as any food you have ever loved. Each stale bite revitalized our weary bones.

"Why does this sandwich taste sooo good?" She asks, laughing until the wine comes out of her nose.

"Because your stonedddd!" I yell, laughing and doing a little jig, barefoot in the sand.

It wasn't long before we had slipped into our sleeping bags, content with the warmth of the wine and each other. The dying embers of the fire bringing the hope of dawn.

Chapter 2

A Spark of Electricity

The sound of the crashing sea woke us slowly, a ray of light peaked its way through the tent flap and although the previous week had been wrought with harsh winds and a steady drizzle, the morning felt surprisingly warm, inviting almost. The good weather and gentle conditions brought a slow start to the day. With the early morning Ionic reds and golds and silvers, the tide rushing in and coming to a gentle halt, lit up with color and foam. Japan and the orient and an endless expanse of ocean were all that were in front of us. We were in no real hurry and the simple relaxed beauty of the California coast made the perfect cup of coffee.

"Hey, do you want to take a quick walk around the area to see what's around? Maybe there's a better spot?" I ask her as she rummages about our things. Looking for something to occupy her morning.

"No, I'm too lazy right now. You go on ahead and I'll just take a little nap." She says smiling and snuggling back into her sleeping bag.

Leaving her to rest and walking barefoot, feeling the frigid pacific curl around my ankles gave me time to think. Our situation still seemed bleak, but there was a sense of adventure on the horizon. For the first time in several weeks there seemed to be a small flame growing. It grew inside the pit of my stomach and kept me warm from our cold reality. It felt like new magic that was just beginning in the world, not yet tested by mortal hands.

Last night with the fire and the waves crashing. It had awoken something inside of me, new ideas were emerging. New visions of what might be next. Initially when we had left New York we were headed for Alaska. But we had left late in the season and our car had taken forever crossing the great divide between coasts. Our goals weren't very clear. Alaska was just a point on a larger map. Maybe we could get jobs there? Or maybe we could build a cabin in the woods and get eaten by a grizzly bear. I can't stress enough how little we had thought it through.

My thoughts were suddenly interrupted by the sound of a guitar, a folky tune with a deep and rich voice singing brightly. I continued towards the sound, winding around the bend of dunes coming closer and closer to what sounded like a mini concert. I had a brief fantasy of mermen singing to the sea. As I approached the bend the scene turned out to be closer to the fantasy than anything else.

Just around the curve and slope of a giant dune a rugged scene opened. Full of scattered boulders and rocky coastline. Close by sat a small cluster of travelers, their hair matted and dreaded, their clothes patched and colorful. From a distance the scene was a reflection of Robin Hood's merry men. There was song and the smell of food cooking over a fire. A short distance away, closer to the beach, two women were dancing naked in the surf.

I continued to walk toward them, doing my best to avert my eyes from the dancing sea nymphs. As I neared a tall gangly kid came running up to me with a big smile on his face and a ragged mutt of a dog followed. "Howdy brother! Come join us if you'd like!"

"Hey man, I'm James. We've got a little camp a few hundred feet up the beach. " I say while shaking his hand.

"Nice to meet ya! I'm Tommy J and this here mutt is Geronimo. What brings you out to this little secret patch of sand?" He asks in a flowing tone. His lanky tanned figure set in almost a dancer's pose. Slender hands stained with soil and smoke. He wore colorful, loose fitting trousers that billowed in the wind. Bare chested and bare chinned. His youthful exuberance made you immediately like him. "Yeah it's nice to meet you. So what are you guys up to? Looks fun." I say with a shy smile.

"You guys have to come join us brother. We're on the road from Tennessee. There's going to be a big party for a few days. Everyone is welcome.

"Our car broke down a few weeks ago and we've just been hitchhiking our way around the coast. We have zero plans, so yeah. We'll definitely join in." I say, excited to bring the news back to Sara.

"There's enough for everyone!" said a man with flowers in his hair. Standing up from an uncomfortable looking yoga pose and doing a small dance in front me and then disappearing afterwards to dance naked with the sea nymphs.

"That's Moonflower. He's a wild one. But yeah grab your stuff and move down here if you'd like. Tons of room. Lots of food and everything else too. We're part of the rainbow family. It's all about community, brother." Tommy J says while waving goodbye and running after his dog.

With a wave I turn to head back towards our camp, I'm eager to share the news with Sara. At the very least we have food for the night. I shuffle through the heavy sand and make my way over the top of the dune to come out to where our little campsite has been set up. Coming up to the rise where I can look down on our camp and a happy scene awaits. With Sara are two other girls who on closer inspection are the naked sea nymphs, this time with loose fitting clothes hanging from their narrow shoulders. Both are deeply tanned with dreadlocked hair adorned with beads.

"Hi, I was just talking with your friend here. We're having a rainbow gathering over the next couple days! You guys should totally come join in." One of the girls says with a drawl and a wasted smile.

"Yeah I just met Moonflower and Tommy J. Looks like a lot of fun." I say while looking at Sara to gauge her reaction. She gives me a quick, quiet look of approval and we agree to meet up with them later. They cheerfully bound away, back into the sea from whence they came.

"So that was Jade and Pumpkin Seed. They seem nice. And maybe a little crazy." She says laughing. Pointing to the area behind the giant dune I tell her about the upcoming party and the group of traveling musicians leading the pack.

"Well, we have nothing better to do. Might as well join in. At least there will be food." I say with a shrug and a laugh. We've never been free spirits like these magical beings that seem to dance with abandon. Lots of travel but always separate from the energy of hippy communions. They have their own hierarchy, just like other social groups. You've got your good ones that are truly on a path and then you have your cult leaders. Everything in between is what these people seemed to represent. And with no money and no real knowledge of our future, joining this merry group of travelers was going to be the best bet we could make.

Deciding to keep our campsite where it was for now, we clambered down the dunes and followed the beach past the sea nymphs and up to the camp where I had met Tommy J. In just the brief time that I had been away there were already two new vehicles parked along the beach to the side of the main camp. Added to the group were both young and old earthy type folk.

Some carried guitars and jimbays and others carried boxes of supplies. A large multi-colored gazebo was being constructed by a motivated handful of the free folk. Moonflower was doing some sort of discombobulated yoga move while sucking in his skinny chest and showing off his ribs like a prized rooster. Tommy J is out in the waves with his pup and the two sea nymphs. You can feel the energy of the camp building. Moonflower spots us hanging out on the periphery and waves us over.

"Howdy campers, come on over and join me for a spell." He drawled, in a smooth southern accent. We shuffled over through the sand and took a seat next to him.

"Those were some pretty sweet moves you were doing Moonflower." I say.

"Yeah, you like that huh? I was just centering my chi. A little yoga never hurt a soul." He reaches into his satchel that hangs across his shoulders and pulls out some tobacco to stuff into an old corn cob pipe and lights it with a match that sends the perfumed smoke wafting across the beach. Flicking the match into oblivion and peering over the pipe at us through squinting eyes.

"So, what's your story? What are your names again? What brings you to this hullabaloo?" He asks, after letting out a massive smoke cloud.

"This is Sara and I'm James. We were on a roadtrip from New York to Alaska but our car exploded a few hundred miles north of here. And now we're just sort of homeless until we can figure out our next move." I say in a sort of humble tone, I'm looking for advice. Or help.

"Excellent. That's the best story I've heard all day. Congratulations!" He shouts the last word and everyone turns around to say to us, "Congratulations!" in unity.

Sara and I exchange looks of bafflement and in a shocked tone I say, "I'm sorry, what? I don't understand."

"I don't expect you to, not yet anyways. You guys are on the precipice of a grand adventure. The truest kind of adventure. Where the real electric magic happens. That's a rare thing these days. The plastic world out there is severely lacking in authenticity." He says, shaking his head and sending his dreads swaying.

"What do you mean by electric magic?" I ask in a skeptical voice. Maybe it wasn't a good idea to come to this strange gathering. A small drum circle has already gathered not far away and shrieks and chants are met with a steady pounding rhythm. It has the feel of some kind of pagan ceremony. Wild and animalistic.

"Electric magic, like lightning, is the current that carries us along life's journey. In various forms it will appear. It only shows itself in the most original of moments." He's whispering now, and looking around suspiciously.

"Some might even call it destiny." He says in a vague tone while waving his corn cob pipe to accentuate his point.

The drum circle had continued to grow and without a word Moonbeam stands and almost as if we had never existed, joins the circle to dance. The drums beat a steady rhythm that awakens something primal in our bellies. Each beat echoing an ancient voice that seemed to come from the very beginning of time. The waves were starting to pick up now. Huge, white capped giants that answered the call of the drums. For a moment I felt the urge to join the circle but held back. The fear had gripped me, I was not ready yet, to jump into the abyss.

Looking at Sara, she was equally enraptured. Her exotic mediterranean eyes danced with the rhythm. I reached over to touch her hand, almost to pull her from a trance. Looking back at me she smiled. A smile so deep and satisfied that it almost scared me. Who was this new Sara? She was shedding her old skin.

I felt like crawling back inside my skeleton and hiding. I was impressed but a hot feeling of jealousy fell into the pit of my stomach with a splash. Followed then by a cold chill of fear that crept up my spine and my knees began to tremble so I stood up quickly and walked away from the group towards the ocean. The sound of the drums were pounding in my chest. My heart and lungs moved with each down beat and felt like both organs were tired of my body and wanted to join with the mob of sweaty dancing bodies. Walking quickly to the water's edge and feeling the cold water swirl around my ankles grounded me and I felt safe again. Sara had gotten up to follow me and was soon by my side.

"Hey, are you ok?" She asks, taking my hand in hers. It's warm and soft and full of life. Her pulse is beating to the pagan rhythms.

"I just got overwhelmed for a second. Had to get away." I say, gulping the fresh sea air down and looking away so she can't see my fear.

"Hey, it's ok. That Moonbeam guy is definitely crazy but this is kind of incredible that we stumbled on this now at this weird time in our life."

"I like what he's saying, but it almost feels like we're falling further into a rabbit hole that I'm not ready for." I say as the drums continue to beat savagely.

"Let's just try and have some fun, maybe forget about our lives for a little while. What do you say?" She says, pulling me back to the ceremony with luminous eyes and a mischievous smile that seems ready for anything. How can I say no, so I follow her back and lose myself in the pounding drum beats. I find myself dancing with Moonbeam. Sara is twirling with the sea nymphs and we drift into oblivion for a little while.

* * *

Later a wave of vans and tie-dyed shirts arrived, a hundred different hilarious characters popping in and out of our view like colorful jack in the boxes. There were musicians and performers. Artists of all types. Fire dancers and naked hippies running and playing in the water. There were multicolored tents set up and people were already tuning their instruments. The drum circle seemed to never stop. A constant, ancient rumble that resounded deep into the night for an entire week. It seemed to be the last great push before the season drove them south. That first morning was the precursor to a wild week. A good turn of events considering the previous ones. But as we all learn in time, good things only last so long. The coming of winter made itself known as the week continued, building and building like a massive gray wave until the inevitable crash.....

Chapter 3

Paychecks and Daydreams

An empty soda can tap, tapped its way across the abandoned parking lot until it snuggled into a ditch in the sand. A harsh wind blew offshore as we huddled in a storm drain looking out over our beach. It was just the two of us now, still lost but with a lilt in our step. We were the last of the season, as the great hippy migration moved south. Gone were the sounds of the drums, the jimbays and the guitars. The dead heads and the phish heads, even the pinheads. Moonbeam and Tommy J had left early, disappearing with the sea nymphs on the third night. They had all left, gone like the season they came with. Winter was here.

"We should head into town to check the post office for your check." Sara said, coming out of a shivering funk whilst huddled over the small fire we had made. We had spent the previous day helping to clean up the mess the rainbow gathering had made. For peaceful, earth loving hippies they sure knew how to leave a mess. We were exhausted. And tired of the sand, that somehow had found its way into every crevice of our bodies and gear. It was even in my teeth and in my eyes and ears. My final paycheck, from what seemed like a long-lost life, a million years before, was supposed to arrive in the post, general delivery. A friend back home in New York had sent it on to us. We had managed to get a hold of him at the library where the internet was free. This was in the days before smartphones and the mystical 5G networks. We had to hike our stinky butts all the way into town and wait for the only computer with internet. You get an hour and if that's not enough, too bad.

We had two goals in mind while surfing the interweb. The first was to find out if our check was on the way. The second to see if we couldn't find a car or van for cheap. It would be better to sleep in a vehicle than on the mean streets of California. We had found a few options but the one we hoped and prayed for was a wild looking, early eighties converted ambulance. A Ford 350 engine and the interior gutted behind the front seats. It looked like some kind of mechanical marshmallow and it immediately struck Sara's eye. Out of our price range but she still took the number down. I was focused on a smaller and equally as ancient Honda that was so affordable it led me to question its value.

After struggling through the freezing beach and up towards the small town of Fort Bragg we made our way to the post office. It was still early in the morning and the doors had just opened. The postal worker was friendly and after showing my ID promptly handed me my letter. The joy and elation was at a fever pitch. Clutching the envelope in my hand as we shuffled out the door like crabs protecting our scavenged goods. Nervously glancing out of the corner of our eyes for the bandits and pickpockets that surely lurked just outside the protected doors.

"Ok, open it. The suspense is killing me." She says as we get out into the parking lot. I slip my thumbnail under the lip and neatly tear open the top of the envelope. Inside I can see the textured check and pulling it out brings a smile that weighs ten thousand pounds. Handing it quickly over to Sara without looking, she unfolds the check for the big reveal.

"What's it say? How much?" I ask nervously, practically chewing my fingernails to a bloody nub.

"Eight hundred dollars and eleven cents! We're rich!" She says with a hoot. We embrace and then do a little Indian war dance while praising the gods for the safe delivery of our salvation. What a difference money can make in the hands of the poor. The sudden compulsive thought to splurge crossed our minds only once as the cheque cashier handed us eight, crisp hundred-dollar bills. Each bill slammed with a resounding crash on the polished table as the teller counted out the exact amount. The teller was an overweight, slightly balding man, with darting beady eyes. There was the suspicious look upon entry, the bell ringing loudly as I pushed open the door. Our huddled masses left in the doorway, and the woman and I in almost rags as we made our way to the counter with bullet proof glass. Suspicion runs deep in the hearts of coastal California locals. There had been too many bums and dirt bags passing through town over the years. Every village has a horror story of a drug addled drifter. After the money is counted and shoved through the slit at the bottom of the glass we scoop it up like treasure and hurry from the glaring eyes.

"I can't believe we're holding this much money. It feels like we're rich." Sara says, shaking her head.

"What do you want to do first?" I ask, looking at her glowing beauty holding the money in disbelief.

"I'm starving. Let's find some food in an actual restaurant."

Outside we reorient ourselves by finding the nearest Mexican restaurant. Life decisions are best made with a margarita and taco in hand. Walking up the concrete sidewalk with the sea to our left and the town to our right we are almost skipping with glee. We had been completely penniless for weeks now. The feeling of having just this small amount of eight hundred dollars was life changing.

After passing a few random shops we come to a cheerful and colorful looking taqueria called Los Gallitos. Mariachi music loudly playing from the kitchen, the counter with the brightly decorated menu displaying images of all the most delicious things a person can consume. In the top corner you see three different types of burritos. Carne Asada, Al Pastor and Carnitas and something called Lengua which we would eventually come to find out was tongue, but it was delicious and I want three, right now, as I'm typing this. There were tacos and enchiladas, chili rellenos and tamales. Soup both hot and cold and many other delectable goodies that make me drool in hunger to think about. Next to the counter is the cold buffet full of pickled chillies and carrots and various salsas of different colors and spice levels. It's a paradise of the senses and a smorgasbord for the taste buds. This is the epitome of all civilization, here in Los Gallitos taqueria.

"Two margaritas, hold the salt and six al pastor tacos Por Favor" I say in an excited tone.

"No problem, take a seat and we'll bring it over." The man behind the counter says. His sweat beaded forehead glistens in the neon signs light and the toothy smile speaks of all the best things to come. He's practically glowing with an angelic light and I have a sudden urge to grab his hand and shake it warmly. This is the owner, the chef and the host. He can sense our desperation for the satiation of the food and drink and he seems to move faster than expected.

Picking a seat next to the window that looks out onto the street we settle in and prepare for the delicious meal to come. First comes the Margaritas, green and citrus scented. They are placed delicately in front of us. The glasses clink against the tiled table. In order to appear civilized we only sip on them. Our shaking hands want so much to just drink them down to the last icy sip but we know that it's best savored with the tacos.

Glancing over at the salsa bar I also make sure to stock up on a generous portion of pickled carrots and jalapeños. Stuffing these into your tacos will add substance and depth. Layered flavors that would surely delight even the most dour of gourmands. Three different flavor packed salsas also adorn both of our trays and they range from mild and delicious to unstable and scorching. The kind of heat that can make a man lose his mind and run blindly into traffic.

The food arrives moments later with great flair. Our man carrying all six tacos and a heaping mound of chips and extra salsa on a tray with one hand. He swings around the corner and in seconds the savory meat filled wraps are steaming in front of our faces. We nod in thanks and dig in. First topping each taco with a pickled carrot or jalapeño and a dollop of the salsas. Folding them carefully into an aerodynamic food vessel, we bring them to their glorious fate. There can be no greater food death than for that of the Oaxacan taco. Each bite is a miracle, a revelation even. The pineapple and the perfectly roasted pork combine to create flavors that transcend this dimension. There is and never will be a comparison. Not a word is spoken between us as we munch and crunch our way through the exotic meal.

Now, with the tacos consumed and the margaritas schwilling in our full stomachs we lean back to think and to discuss. For the last several weeks we had felt the necessity of shelter and transportation. At first it was romantic, being a leather tramp and on the road.

After a time though it starts to wear on you, like last week's underwear. There is only so much one can take of crazed meth freaks and self righteous hippies. It's fun when the drugs are coursing through your veins and the drum beat finds a rhythm in your soul. Soon enough the trip ends and you're left with cold feet and the ever prevailing chill of California's coastal climate.

"Let's find a place for you to call the guy with the ambulance," Sara says quietly. Looking across the table with those same fiery eyes I had seen days before. Her mind was already starting to turn with the possibilities.

"We don't have a thousand dollars though, he'll probably say no." I respond with a grumpy taco burp that permeates the small corner of the restaurant. "What about that Honda?

"Gross, let's go. Just try and see if he'll negotiate. And that Honda sucks. We should really try for the van." She says, waving her tiny hand in front of her face in disgust.

We waddle out of Los Gallitos with a delighted wave and two thumbs up to the chefs. Back out on the mean streets of this tiny coastal town we make our way to the gas station across the street with a row of pay phones just outside. Just outside is a mumbling meth head, kicking cans in the direction of the phones. It's best to wait it out, we think. No reason to enter into that lunatic space. The creature decides he's best needed behind the station where the other scag barons dwell and we move quickly across the street. I punch in the numbers written down in Sara's notebook and drop two quarters in the slot. The phone rings three times and a booming voice greets me.

"Hello, Aldon here" In a voice that reminds me of a fifty year old roofing contractor who's powerful voice could cut through the sound of industrial equipment.

"Hey there, this is James. We got your number off Craigslist for the van for sale" I say with as much buyers confidence as I can muster. A voice that says, "I know what cars are and how they work so don't rip me off". It probably came out shaking and squeaking like an old rusty door hinge.

"Yeah sure, c'mon on down to my place and you can have a look" He says gruffly. He gives us the address and directions and we hang up the phone. Excited and nervous we walked towards the street that, according to Aldon, was not too far from the gas station where we started.

"God I hope we can get this van, It would change everything." She says with eternal hope in a tiny voice.

I'm still uncertain, because nothing good ever happens when you truly need it. The good things always come when you're warm and comfortable, somewhere safe when the bugs aren't biting and the wind isn't blowing.

"Well see my love, we'll see." I say without much in the way of expectations. Following the main road past a few more shops and then on past the harbor. The sidewalk is old, maybe as old as the town. Gazing over at Sara as we shuffle quickly down the road and a look of hope shines from her eyes.

"You never know. Our luck might just be changing." She says, picking up speed with excitement.

Chapter 4

Aldon

Making our way down the boulevard and taking the second left, following it down to the end where a tidy little cul-de-sac rests peacefully. The avenue is shaded by big old California oak trees that have lost almost all of their golden leaves. A few still hang on by a thread, waving to us as we walk towards the big blue house, third on the right.

The sprawling front yard is cheery, a few cars scattered along its long driveway that leads to the back yard. An overgrown lawn with various junk strewn about and an open garage door filled to the brim with exotic mechanical bits and bobs. Spent engine blocks and old used up carburetors, a butcher block bench cluttered with chisels and various hammers, nails and the broken teeth of fifty different spokes, wrenches and chains. Behind the house, you can see the crowns of tall redwood trees that open up to the forest that reaches up into the mountains.

"Ahoy there!" a voice calls. The kind of voice that rings out into the dark night to check for the bad things. The kind of voice that can lead you back to the light when you've strayed too far.

Father Christmas himself emerges from the dark nether regions of the garage. A mountain of a man, in his late sixties with a full and flowing white beard. A bald and be spotted head with sparkling blue eyes and a pair of tinted Windsor glasses placed jauntily at the end of his nose. His belly is made of jelly and steel and shrapnel and good bbq. With purpose he walks over to us and extends a hand made of stone and sand.

"Hi there, I'm James and this is Sara, we spoke on the phone a moment ago." I say, after he releases my hand from his crushing grip.

"Ah yes, the couple that wants to take a look at the old ambulance. Well she's right down this way, follow me and watch out for old Jake." He says and trundles down the long drive way towards the back. Old Jake turns out to be an ancient and lazy springer spaniel with a limp in his gate. He trots over to us with a wagging tail and begging eyes. I laugh and give his old head a scratch as we pass by his perch.

We turned a corner to the massive backyard and there, alone, amongst the overgrown weeds and shrubs of a matching unruly yard was the most beautiful vehicle we had ever seen. From a distance you could almost call it a giant marshmallow for it was massive and puffy. Hospital white and rounded along the top to add headspace. Two red lights spaced evenly apart acted as the siren lights. Long glazed over by the salt air and other harsh elements. She was a mess but she was still beautiful to us.

"It may look like shit but she's got a great engine and all of the parts are working. Except the siren of course" He says with friendly confidence.

He waves us on to suggest we explore further. Opening the broad sliding door we peer into the empty space. It looks to us like a clean canvas. A large flat space where various instruments and shelves used to be. Basically a cavernous area full of potential. The driver and passenger seat are open to the back and the passenger seat swivels to face the back if you want it to. Sara climbs in and fiddles about, pretending to know what she's doing. I ask to see the engine and he promptly opens the drivers door and pops the hood. Gazing into the dusty old space it's hard to imagine that it's the engine he described but no sooner than I had thought that, he turns the key and she roars to life. The big V8 engine combusting and exploding in a sound of glory and power.

"Alright so what do you guys think?" He asks with twinkling eyes and a small smile. His friendly nature is layered with that steel determination. This is not a man who will haggle lightly.

"She looks great and perfect for what we need. We're travelers and would like to fix her up to live in. There's just one problem…" I say with as much humility as I can muster.

"Oh, what's the problem?" He asks hesitantly

"I only have six hundred and fifty dollars." I say with the hope he doesn't know about the other hundred and twenty left in my wallet.

"Well I can't get rid of it for that, I can do eight hundred and fifty and that's got to be my final offer. A van like this usually goes for way more. I just want to get it out of my yard" He says, frustrated.

"I totally get that, the truth is sir, we just don't have much more than six hundred and fifty. We still need to get it insured and put gas in the car and to be honest we only have about seven hundred and fifty to our name." I say with desperation.

"Jesus, seven hundred and fifty dollars? Why do you only have that much? What's your story, are you guys homeless or something?" He asks not unkindly. His eyes have lost their steel and you can see concern in the twinkling depths.

"Sort of, our car broke down on our way north last month. We have been on a cross country adventure heading to Alaska but the weather got in the way. We've just been camping and trying to find our direction." I reply with a little shame and a little pride.

"Oh wow, you guys are in trouble then. I can't get rid of this van for anything less than 800. I'm really taking a hit here. What about your parents? Any chance they can help?" He's being gentle now. He can sense our predicament. Sara looks like she's on the edge of tears. It's the first time we've told our story to a normal human and not a fellow hippy bum.

"Our parents wouldn't even help if we asked. We're trying to figure this out on our own. Is there anything we can do to lower the price" I say looking around at the untidy yard and various piles of rubbish strewn about.

"Any chance I can do some work for you? I've worked landscaping and other labor jobs before? I know it's a lot to ask but we're a little desperate here. I really need to find some kind of shelter before winter takes off" I'm pleading now, almost begging. I consider dropping to my knees to pray to this gentle old man's generosity.

He scratches his bald head and takes a step back. Looking around and thinking. We quietly stand together with our heads down hoping for a miracle.

"Ok, Let me go talk this over with my wife. You guys seem like good kids. I'd like to help you out but I need the big boss's permission." He says with an awkward smile.

"Just hang out here and give me a second." He says and then turns around to head back to the house.

We look at each other with a bit of sadness and hope. I take her into my arms and we cling to each other for a moment. Silently I pray to all the gods for mercy. Please I pray, please let this man take pity on us. If I can just get this van I'll never be bad again. I'll be a perfect saint from here on out, God please help us.

I say all of this silently as we hold hands and keenly gaze at the back door waiting for Aldon to reappear. I can hear a dog barking from inside the house and minutes later a short and plump lady emerges from the screen door at the back. She's waving at us now and her face is full of wrinkles and smiles. Hope begins to warm our bones just like the margarita and tacos. She is of sturdy design, short hair and big hoop earrings. Her eyes are old and wise and have the slanted look of Asian descent, or maybe even Eskimo.

"Hello! My husband says you guys are a little stuck? My name is Sharon." She says, crossing the distance between the house and the van in seconds. Her smile is warm and generous but also hesitant. I can sense that she's reading our faces, searching for any evil.

"Hi, My names James and this is Sara. Yeah we've been on a pretty wild adventure recently and we'd really appreciate anything you can do or suggest." I say with the earnestness of a pious monk.

She gazes deep into our eyes and gives us a knowing look.

Aldon approaches now with a second small dog in tow. It's one of those unfortunate lap dogs that looks like a walking mop. He almost steps on it and in doing so the dog lets out a small YIP. Scooping the dog up he joins his wife and they both look at each other quickly. She nods and he smiles.

"Alright guys, if you'd like you can camp in the van tonight and we can give you work for a couple days to make up for the missing amount. Maybe even put a few extra dollars in your pocket before you go." He says with a warm smile.

"We were hippies in the sixties and we know what it's like to be on an adventure" Sharon says with a joyous smile.

The weight of the world is suddenly lifted and we almost squeal with happiness. "Thank you so much, I can't tell you how much we appreciate this. We will be happy to do whatever is needed." Sara says unexpectedly. Usually she's too shy to interact with people but her happiness is un-contained today.

"That's quite alright, why don't you come with me and I'll show you the garden and a few other household projects I've been meaning to tackle." She says and grabs Sara's little hand and sweeps her off to the house.

"Alright young man, come with me to the garage. I've got piles of work and I'm actually a little glad you guys came along. We're too old to do some of this stuff and our kids have long since moved on. How are you with mechanics?" He asks with hope in his voice.

"To be honest sir, I've only ever changed my oil and brake pads but I'm a fast learner and willing to get my hands dirty." I say with shaky confidence.

We walk back down the long lane to the front of the house and garage. Inside the garage smells like oil and wood shavings. Two old project cars are settled in their own mess with various parts, tubes, bits and bobs strewn about. The first car I can immediately tell is an old Mustang convertible. The other is some kind of

Chevy that I don't recognize. Both look amazing in their broken down squalor. The hood of the Mustang is popped and a massive cavernous space is where the engine block should be. Various wires and dangly bits are protruding and it looks like an intimidating job for even the most seasoned mechanic.

"Had to replace the engine in my 67' Mustang. I'm picking the engine up today from the shop. I'll need your help to hoist it into place and to connect all the dots. Can you manage something like that." He asks with a gruffness in his voice.

"Yeah just tell me what to do and I'll do it." I say eagerly.

"Ok good that's what I like to hear." Let's go check on the girls and then I'll get you to come with me to the shop."

Making our way into the house through the garage there is a total shift in appearance. The untidy mess of the garage and yard is replaced by a neat and organized kitchen that opens out into a cozy and clean living area. A big comfortable couch and a reclining easy chair sits in front of one of those old, massive TVs made of wood and glass. Shelves line the walls all filled to the brim with books and trinkets. In between the shelves are old family photos in neat simple frames. Shag carpet meets the linoleum of the kitchen floor and Aldon leans over to take his shoes off before stepping onto the carpet. He looks at me to do the same and I do. Stepping out onto the plush carpet and curling my toes like I used to at my grandma's house when I was little. I can hear the girls chatting in a distant room and Aldon leads me through the living room and down a hall that has several closed doors and one open. The room is a study of sorts. Large comfortable chairs and a big mahogany desk. Behind the desk is Sara, all smiles holding a big glass of red wine and laughing. Sharon is sitting across from her and also holding both a wine glass and the bottle. She turns to look as we enter.

"Well it's official Aldon, we're going to adopt these two straight away." She says with a laugh.

"Hey, let's see how this one handles the work out in the garage first." He says with a smile.

"And what happened to the two of you working on the garden. I didn't realize it was wine o'clock yet."

"Hush, we're just getting to know each other. Sara is from New York! Remember that trip we took out to Woodstock and the city? We'll work on the garden tomorrow. What are you fellas up to?" Her sweet face is full of mirth and laughter. I can tell by the look on Sara's face that she feels comfortable and safe and a warmth spreads over me that not even a glass of wine can reproduce.

"I'm going to take James to the shop to pick up the engine and we'll try and work on the Ford tomorrow morning. What do you say Jay? Are you ready to go to the shop with me?" Aldon laughs.

"Yes sir, let's do it!" I say with gusto.

"Don't call me sir, I work for a living." He responds.

"Call me Aldon or Ol' Fatso or whatever. I was an NCO not an officer." He says pointing to a picture of a much younger man in a Marine Corps uniform. Above the picture is a folded flag and a shining sword mounted on a wooden plaque.

"We met when Aldon came back from Vietnam in 69'. We were so young then." Sharon says with a hint of nostalgia in her voice.

"I was in the Army actually." I say, hoping to impress him.

"Well, we won't fault you for that." He says with a laugh.

"C'mon lets get this over with. Are you girls going to be ok without us?"

"Pshh, go and do your man things. Sara and I will be just fine." She says with a wave of her hand. She turns back to Sara and the two of them start clucking like an old pair of hens. We leave just as Sharon tops up Sara's wine glass.

Exiting the house through the big wooden front door we jump into the old truck parked just outside the garage and start down the road. The tape deck turns on, blasting the familiar sounds of the Grateful Dead and I feel at ease. I roll down my window and put my arm out to feel the breeze. Aldon looks on and drives in silence.

"You like The Dead?" He finally asks.

"I love them! I'm still mourning Jerry." I say sagely.

"Well, he did his thing and left the world with a lot of awesome music. You can't mourn someone who completed their circle. It was just his time." He says with a hint of sadness in his voice. I imagine all that this old man has been through. Vietnam, the sixties, life. I hope I can be like him someday. Settled in an old cul-de-sac with big oak trees and a shady backyard. For a moment I get a glimpse of my imaginary future. Sara is full of wrinkles and sweet gray hair and I'm an old stooped man with a booming laugh and a twinkle in my eye. Why not? I think.

The drive doesn't take long as we pass Los Gallitos taco shop and the gas station with the moaning scag barons. Driving just a bit further and there's an old garage with a backyard that looks out onto the Pacific. Pulling in quickly off the highway another old man emerges from the confines of the garage. Browned skin, a thick black mustache speckled with white and an old pair of blue stained overalls. Aldon rolls down his window and shouts at the man.

"Hey, you lazy old wetback, is my engine ready to go or what." Aldon says with a smile.

"It's here and ready to go you potato head mother fucker. It's been sitting here for days just like I told ya." The man laughs.

We exit the truck and come around to greet him. Aldon points to me and says, "This is my new assistant. James. He was in the Army but we won't make fun of him for that. This is Henry. Henry and I go way back." Aldon says with a laugh that shakes his jelly belly.

"Way back to the beginning of time, young man. I still remember when this Irish asshole was shitting himself in the jungle. He likes to act tough but he's just an old teddy bear." He says, shaking my hand with an iron grip.

Henry leads us into the shop where a hoist is attached with chains to a shiny new engine block. Eight metal pistons in the shape of a V. It looks mean and young and ready to party. Aldon walks around it to inspect it and seems satisfied. He snorts, "Well it looks ok. Lets hope you didn't fuck it up this time." He says with good natured humor.

"Ha, let's hope I don't see you back in here after you forget to put oil in it." Henry says with mock annoyance.

Aldon tosses me the keys to the truck and tells me to back it up to the engine so they can hoist it into the bed. I trot back to the truck while the two old men walk into the office to settle up. Turning the engine and carefully backing the truck up to the block I can't help but smile at these two old codgers. You can tell they are good friends by the way they banter and laugh. It feels good to see two people so connected. In this ever changing world of insanity we forget that there used to be viable communities of various cultures all getting along in their own dogged way.

I turn off the engine and stand next to the hoist waiting for the two of them to return. Looking through the glass window of the office I see the two of them looking at me and smiling. Henry waved me inside and I hurried to the door.

"Aldon just told me of you and your wife's situation. We've all been there before young man. If you'd like I've got some extra work around the shop that needs doing. If you're keen and willing to get your hands dirty." He says with kindness.

"I'd appreciate any work I can get. We'd like to save up for a big trip up north in the Spring." I say with a smile on my face.

"Well, when you're done at Aldon's come on back here and we'll sort you out." He says.

The day moves by quickly now. We hoist the new engine into the back of the truck and shake hands with Henry. He walks back to his office with an overhead wave just as Aldon pulls out with two taps to the horn. The car rumbles its way down the two lane coastal highway and there is that certain pleasant feeling of warmth spreading through my soul. Just a couple good ol' boys going to go home and work on a classic car. For a moment everything is right in the world and I have hope that tomorrow will be better than yesterday. Aldon turns up the volume and the Grateful Dead sing songs about trucking and the clean ocean air caresses my hair and face.

"When we get home, we'll take the engine out of the truck and put it in the garage next to the Mustang. Then we'll see what trouble the girls have gotten into." He says, with a voice full of wisdom and jolly mirth.

"Sounds good to me." I say with the enthusiasm of a six year old who finally gets to help his old man with the car.

"Don't think it's all going to be this easy. I'm not going to pay you for just sitting around." He laughs with his jelly belly.

"It's getting late though and there's no use starting half way through the day. We'll get you going on the yard tomorrow and then we'll drop the engine later in the day." He says with the final note accentuated with an Ay like your in the deep south and your drooling a little.

"No problem at all, we really appreciate this Aldon. It's going to help us get on down the road." I say softly.

The truck is turning down the lane that is lined with those glorious old oaks and in two seconds were reversing up the long driveway and settling directly outside the open garage door. The girls must have heard us coming from down the street because they're sitting on chairs just next to the garage in the tall grass of the overgrown lawn. Sara is laughing her sweet, joyous laugh and Sharon is smiling and telling a story with one hand waving freely whilst the other loosely holds a half empty glass of wine.

"You see Jay, I knew they'd get into trouble if we left them for too long". Aldon laughs.

"Did you guys have a good time?" I ask.

"Oh yes, Sharon has been telling me stories of the sixties and it's great." Sara says with an intoxicated giggle.

"Ok, boys and girls, it's time I started dinner and then we'll make plans for tomorrow. Sara, do you want to help me in the kitchen and I'll finish that story about the time Aldon tried to trick me into marrying him the first time." She laughs with that sweet matronly laugh that only comes with a hundred or so years of wisdom and experience.

"Yeah sure, I can't wait," Sara says with a laugh and a mischievous look towards Aldon.

"Hmmph, I didn't try to trick her, I just merely suggested she'd be lucky to have me." Aldon says with a smile.

After the girls leave, clucking their way back into the house. Arms flailing about holding half drunk wine glasses, Aldon and I head to the back of the truck and roll out the hoist. He points to the back of the truck and wordlessly suggests I wrap the chains around and under the engine block. It's a no brainer job and I only mess it up a couple times. His patience seems veiled with typical old man annoyance and I laugh to myself. Once the thick, braided chains are perfectly placed I jump down and the old man easily hoists the engine into the air swinging it around to rest gently on a sturdy table placed near the front end of the car.

"Well leave her here to rest before we drop it in tomorrow." He says with simple satisfaction.

"Now, do you want a beer? Yeah I bet you do, go and grab a couple from the fridge at the back of the garage."

I wade through the clutter and open the fridge to reveal floor to ceiling beer. Cheap, good American beer. Budweiser, Pabst blue ribbon, Coors light. This is a fridge that has never been disgraced with imports or craft beer. I imagine Aldon and Henry disparaging anyone that would even consider asking for a Heineken or Corona. I grab two cans of the Pabst and make my way back to where Aldon has roosted in the same spot occupied by the ladies minutes before. It's a compact little circle of lawn chairs and in the middle a rusty but usable fire pit. I hand him the ice cold beer and sit down next to him. He holds the beer away from him and with gusto, cracks it open sending spray and goodness everywhere. I also crack mine open with relish and he looks on with approval.

"So what's your plan once you leave here with the van?" He asks quietly.

"To be honest, we don't really have one." Our original plan had been to drive north to Alaska. We'd find work at a ski resort or hunting lodge and then go from there. Now that the weather has changed and the northern passage to Alaska becoming increasingly less passable we really had no idea of what was next."

"Well, you need a plan. You can't just go through life forever like this. It's fun while it lasts but eventually you're just moving against the wind."

"For a long time now it just seems like we've been wandering with no real direction. Once we have the van it will at least be a home base that we can live and work out of." I say, hoping he understands.

He doesn't respond with words, just glances over at me and our eyes meet. His both ancient and young and mine as naïve and searching as ever before. He kicks a few logs into the pit and starts to build a fire wordlessly. Before long a healthy mound of starter and old sticks and broken bits of lumber are piled high. He leans back and fishes around for a book of matches in his overall jean pockets. Finding them with a grunt he opens the book and flicks a small match into the base of the fire pit. Magically it only takes one and the fire begins to grow and climb and embrace the small heap of kindling. He nudges the metal fire pit to give it a little shake and the fire roars to life. We sit like that for a while and drink in the warmth of the early evening with the cold beers. Pretty soon it's time for another and this time he gets up and heads to the garage. He rummages around for a little while and returns with two more cans and a small metal container that looks like it once held mints or hard candies.

"I take it you smoke weed." He says as he opens the container to reveal pungent green and a few crinkled papers.

"Yes, we both do." Are the words that come out of my mouth, although I fantasize about throwing some old two bit saying out like, 'Does a bear shit in the woods'. Something that an old badger like this guy would appreciate. I crack open my beer in silence and watch out of the corner of my eye as he expertly begins to roll a joint with one hand.

"So, have you ever worked with weed before?" He asks cautiously, in a hushed tone.

"Actually just a few weeks ago we were on a short trim job up in Arcata. We trimmed a few pounds for this renegade hippy living in the redwoods." I say proudly.

He grunts out a quick laugh and lights the expertly rolled joint with a match flicking the dead stick into the fire pit.

"Well, I'm not just talking about trimming. That's the easy part. Have you ever actually worked with the plant itself?" He asks with a little edge in his voice that means business. "No sir I haven't. But we've wanted to for a long time."

"What did I tell you about that sir shit, my name is Aldon son."

"Sorry about that, it's just a habit." I say nervously.

He takes two or three deep drags off the joint and passes it to me letting out a small cough before releasing a massive cloud of smoke that wafts out into the twinkling evening.

"That's alright, listen I'm going to be straight with you. I could also use help with some plants I have in the back. It would be enough work to set you up for a while, plus the van. Do you think you'd be up for something like that?" He asks quickly and with a degree of suspicion and anticipation.

"Yeah we'd love to do something like that. We'd have zero problems. Just tell us what to do and we'll do it." I say eagerly.

"That's the answer I was hoping for. I'm guessing Sharon is asking Sara the same question inside right now. You both seem like decent kids. But you'd better not get any ideas of fucking us over. We don't take kindly to thieves or cheats out here." He says gruffly.

I don't respond because a response isn't what he's looking for and I take two or three big drags of the sweet and sticky green. Letting out an equally large cloud of pungent smoke. I pass the joint back to him and nod quietly after our eyes meet.

"That's really good stuff." I say, while letting out a thunderous cough that shakes my whole body. He starts to laugh and some ease and peace re-enters our small circle. It's as if he's asked the big question he was waiting to ask all day and now that it's done we can return to our jovial ways. A few minutes later and a few more coughs and tokes and sips from the beer and the front screen door opens with a bang and out pours the two girls giggling again like best friends.

"So did you ask him yet you old coot. Sara has given me the thumbs up from my end." She says with a tone of mirth and mischief in her voice.

"Yes, yes woman. The young man is ready and willing to go. I told him we'd give them the chance to prove themselves." He says gruffly.

"Pshh his bark is worse than his bite honey, don't you worry about him. Just show up and do a good job and he'll be singing your praise in no time." Sharon says all of this while quickly snatching the joint out of Aldons hand and taking two short drags before passing it to Sara.

"Alright let's get everyone fed and bedded down for the night. We start bright and early in the morning." Aldon says while struggling to stand, knees popping, back crunching. He waddles towards the door and beckons the rest of us to follow.

A pleasant meal follows. Roasted vegetables and chicken stacked high on our plates. A few glasses of wine and a quick grab of blankets and pillows and an old mattress to throw in the back of the van. Aldon looks like a happy old grandpa again as he's saying goodnight to us and closing the sliding door with a gentle bang. I look over at Sara because it's the first time we've been alone in hours and I ask.

"So what do you think? Is it safe? Is Sharon cool?" I ask in a flurry of tired excitement.

"She's amazing and super funny and nice. I think we somehow landed in the perfect place. They are just old hippies growing weed. We need to do the best job we can so that we can make a nice chunk of money."

"I agree. Aldon is actually a really nice guy. He's abrupt like that because he needs to be. You never know who people are until you test the waters for a minute. Also his friend Henry offered us work after we're done here. Not sure what kind of work but we should take what we can get."

We make the bed and snuggle up in our new home. The van seems massive from the back. Cavernous with our little mattress and nothing else. You can see where the old instruments and shelves that held medicines and machines to save lives once sat. For only a moment it feels kind of creepy to think of all the people once stuffed in the back on their way to something tragic or sad. Those thoughts are fleeting as we drift off to sleep with the outside sound of autumn crickets and a small wind blowing through the trees, rocking the van ever so slightly. This is our new home, we think as our eyes close with a thud. Dreams take us and our big day of adventures draws to a close.

Chapter 5

In the Valley of the Garden of Abundance

Morning came quietly, with the peaceful chirp of early birds. A soft breeze whistled through the side door and our huddled masses began to stir. First one eye and then the other opened, then a yawn and a stretch.

The van was now illuminated by the light streaming through the front windows and the van appeared even larger than the night before. We had slept easily on the old mattress that Aldon and Sharon had supplied. That and our sleeping bags and our things already scattered about added a homely feel to the empty machine. My movements revive Sara and we look at each other silently for a moment.

"I was worried all of this was a dream and that I'd wake up back in the tent on the beach." She murmurs.

"No, I think this is all very real." I say with a small sigh.

I rummage about until I find my shirt and get dressed quickly. Throughout all of our travels and itinerant work I've always made it a point to be up before the boss. For all of my many faults being late is rarely one. Sara had slept in her clothes so we're basically ready as we slide open the side door to survey our surroundings. Just outside in the early morning pearly light you can make out the backyard facing the house. On the other side of the van is a larger expanse that disappears into a stand of young redwood trees and great clumps of manzanita. That must be where the plants are, I think.

Trying our best to be quiet we get out of the van and mill about, waiting for our benefactors to arrive. The cool and clean ocean air mixed with the pine and redwoods of the back yard bring an enviable scent. It is the cleanest smell I have ever enjoyed. Some future billionaire would be wise to find a way to bottle this air, I think. Bottle it and sell it to the city dwelling scum who suffer for oxygen.

We shake our legs and pinch ourselves to get all of the kinks out and to get the blood flowing. What seems like an eternity only turns out to be a few minutes when the back door of the house slides open and out emerges a cheery and fresh faced Aldon. His glasses perched at the end of his nose and a straw hat on top of his head. And with a Cheshire grin says, "Good morning campers! Are you guys ready to work?". He says in a mock Clark Griswold voice. His smile is infectious and we can't help but give out a little "Whoop"!

"Alright that's what I like to hear. James why don't you come with me, we're going to water the plants first thing. Sara dear, Sharon needs your help in the kitchen for now. We'll have you out in the garden later in the afternoon." Aldon says all of this with his hands waving and powerful legs carrying him through the tall grass towards the back stand of trees. I give Sara a quick kiss and she heads inside the house as I turn to follow the man with the straw hat and the big bushy beard.

Walking quickly behind him we leave the large back yard and enter into the sweet darkness of the forest. We push past the tangle of manzanita and brush which opens out into a tidy little path that leads through the stand of redwoods. Tufts of perfect grass and delicious ferns line the trail and the redwoods, still in their stage of infancy tower above us. The clean smell of the woods is almost nicer than the ocean breeze and everything smells ancient and earthy. We continue to walk in silence for another few minutes until we come to a large opening in the forest, revealing a pleasant meadow and a small stream. The stream is closest to us and beyond the stream and in the center of the meadow are six tidy rows of head high marijuana plants.

"Ok, so here they are, let me introduce you first. Ok girls, this is James, he's going to be helping me for the next few days." He says directly to the plants in the first row. I must have a smirk or a look of confusion, "Hey don't judge, you've got to talk to your plants. Show them you love them." He says defensively.

"Hey I'm not judging, I'd do the same if I had a patch." I say with a smile. Aldon then waves me over to the corner of the patch where a hundred gallon barrel with a hose sticking out of it sits. The hose is connected to the top and winds down into a neat and tidy coil. "First we add some food to the water, grab that jug labeled big buds and add two capfuls." He starts to uncoil the hose as I twist off the lid of the barrel and add two caps of foul smelling liquid to the crystal clear water. 'Come over here and start at the end and water at the base. Evenly distribute all of the water in the barrel throughout the patch.' Aldon says sternly. Walking away to leave me to the watering he goes to a small shed at one of the corners of the square plot, I can hear him rummaging about and muttering to himself. All of this brings a massive grin to my face. Here I am, just a day after getting paid, finding a van and a job. It's incredible how fast your fortunes can change. I would do well to remember that in the future when things get hard again, I think to myself.

Watering each vibrant plant takes time, your mind begins to wander. The plants themselves stand tall at almost six feet from base to crown and as bushy as a Christmas tree. Chunky, swollen buds poke out of the shrubbery to reveal heavily crystalled, tightly packed clumps and the whole plant soaked in the most incredible perfume. The perfume of a fresh marijuana plant is something very special and difficult to compare to almost any other crop. Each plant also produces an enormous amount of oxygen so the whole area has the freshest air imaginable. The sweet, heady almost tangy smell of the weed coupled with the loamy earth and surrounding forest is a smell not soon forgotten by whoever might be lucky enough to experience the moment.

Getting to the end of the row I had almost forgotten that Aldon was still in the shed. A loud shout and a bang resounded from inside. Quickly dropping the hose and rushing over to the shed door to find Aldon flat on his back with a shelving unit on top of him. Bottles of plant feed, sacks of soil and various hoses and connectors are strewn about the small shack and Aldon sitting underneath it all with a shy smile of embarrassment. "Well this is the shit that happens when you get old. Don't let it happen to you. It's hell." He says meekly. I immediately start pulling the rubble off of him and help him to his feet. Brushing himself off he lets out a laugh. "Well we're off to a good start J. How's the watering coming?"

"I've just finished the first row, five more to go." I say cheerfully.

"Alright then, best get back to it, I'll clean this mess up." He says, back to business.

It was nice to see Aldon in such a vulnerable way, it made him just a little more human. My admiration for him only grew as the morning continued. Following the watering, we had various other chores to complete. To start we had to check that the PVC pipes that filled the water tanks were still in a good position to capture the water from the stream. Sometimes animals can knock them about. It's all about gravity, Aldon says, it's as simple as making sure the water can move freely downhill to the barrels. Free water is essential in this business, he says several times. We find that the induction hose has been knocked out of the stream and we position it back under a few rocks to keep it steady. Early morning shifted its warmth to late morning and the sun has started to appear over the crown of the trees surrounding the meadow. The plants are glistening in the sunshine now, each plant covered in perfect orbs of dew. The five fingers of each leaf stretch out to receive the first warmth of the day in ecstasy. In my mind I can hear them all sighing in relief, having been fed and filled with life giving light.

Our next chores are to spend a few minutes trimming each plant. Taking off some of the dead leaves and allowing light to reach the inner sections of the crowded plant. Everything is done in the tidiest of ways. Aldon demanded I bring a bag along with me to throw the excess leaves into once I'm done trimming. "It's for the compost bin and I don't like a messy space, neither do the girls." He says with a matter of fact tone. So far the morning has passed in optimal silence. Neither of us need to say anything as we complete our various chores. A couple hours pass and the sun has reached its midpoint and the little sparkling meadow has started to heat up. Little armies of flying insects buzz about, collecting pollen and other bits of vegetative magic. Aldon appears just as I'm finishing the last row with a lit joint and a smile on his face.

"You're doing a good job Jim, I think this is going to work out just fine. Let's take a break. Follow me, I want to show you something cool." He says while passing me the joint. He walks off without waiting for me to respond and I quickly follow. Leading me further into the forest away from both his home and the meadow we struggle for a moment to get past a barrier of manzanita. Pushing our way through we find ourselves in an old growth redwood forest. Ferns, light shrubbery and the occasional massive stump of an old tree adorn the forest floor and then all around us the towering, ancient giants. For a moment it feels like we've descended into the Jurassic period. Surely a dinosaur once roamed these woods, or maybe still does.

"This is the edge of our property." Aldon says, with a grand gesture. Two giant redwoods whose circumference was wider than a New York City apartment cluster close together surrounded by the emerald darkness of the forest. The trees with their chunky bark in massive lines that shoot straight into the sky for hundreds of feet. Aldon makes his way over to a low cut stump, the remnants of ancient, greedy loggers and sits down to have a few more puffs of the joint. "Sometimes I just like to come out to this spot and have a nice long think. Helps to clear my mind." Aldon says, more to himself than to me. He seems lost in space now as if I'm just another part of the forest. Absentmindedly he passes me the joint and gestures for me to take a seat next to him to sit in quiet and observe the stillness of the forest.

Time passes and the joint burns slowly down to just a little nub that burns the fingers while being hit. I offer Aldon another hit and he shakes his head no. I stomp it out underfoot and get up to stretch. "This is one of the nicest places I've been in a while Aldon, thank you for showing it to me." I say in the hopes that the silence will be broken. We've seemingly been sitting for a long time and it's starting to feel awkward. My voice pulls him out of his silent reverie and he glances with small annoyance in my direction. "What's your hurry young man, are you already eager to get back to work?" He says with a little humor in his voice. I let out a nervous laugh and shrugged my shoulders. We continue to sit in silence listening to the small woodland creatures scurrying about when all of a sudden a loud rustle in the manzanita behind us causes us to turn around in alarm. From out of the tangle of the gnarled blood red trees comes old Jack. His matted fur tangled with briars and stickers. Rushing up to his master he jumps up to lick Aldon's face and to give me a suspicious glare. "Hey there old boy, where did you come from huh? Did mom let you out? Must be time for us to head back for Lunch." Aldon says with a smile. "Alright J, let's head back, the women folk are probably ready for us now. Thanks for enjoying this space with me." I smile in return and pet old Jake, "It's really a sweet spot, I'd like to come back here again." I say. Aldon grunts in approval and quietly begins to lead the way back towards the little meadow and then beyond back to the house. The walk back seemed shorter than the walk out and before we know it we're within sight of the backyard and in seconds at the back sliding door in time for Sara to pop out of the house with a large tray piled high with food. "Hi, Sharon said to bring this out and set it up on the picnic table." She says shyly to Aldon. "That's just perfect dear, go ahead and bring it out and I'll meet you guys in a second." He says kindly. We walk together to the table and settle in to wait for our hosts.

A few moments later Sharon and Aldon appear from the house, each carrying jugs of sweet tea and plates. In seconds the picnic table is set and plates are piled high with various sandwiches and mounds of ruffled potato chips. The sweet tea tinkles in our glasses as we get ready to pounce on the food. Sara is beaming in her sweet, secret way which tells me that her and Sharon have been having a pleasant morning.

"Well, dear, Sara is quite the talent on the sewing machine. She's already repaired both of the curtains in the living room and is already working on the dress I ripped last year." Sharon says with pride. "After lunch we're going to work on the garden and maybe run into town to go grocery shopping."

"Sounds good, Jay and I are going to work on the car for a while and maybe tidy up the garage a bit." Aldon says with his mouth half full of tuna sandwich. Washing it down with some sweet tea he looks over at me and says, "I can tell you don't really know your way around an engine, son, but you can at least hold the flashlight." He says jokingly. I let out a small laugh and a shrug. He's smiling now and I can tell he's getting used to us. The tension of the day before seems long gone and it feels like home for a moment. The sandwiches are all perfectly prepared. Cut in triangles, no crust and piled onto one of those party platters you see in old movies. Tuna, turkey and egg salad. The girls had spent the entire early morning chatting and making lunch. We all had a few corners and a handful of chips, washing it all down with that perfect sweet tea as the early afternoon sun washed down on us through the branches of old trees. Old Jake was fast asleep at my feet as I got up to throw the paper plate into the bin. My movements startled him and he let out a half asleep growl to remind me of his presence. Gingerly, moving around him, I toss my bits into the trash and settle down next to Sara who is still munching away. Aldon has already finished his plate and makes a gesture for us to move towards the garage and the mustang. Sara glances up at me with a half smile and silently lets me know she loves me.

Rising up eagerly to follow Aldon I can feel the excitement. Like two kids on Christmas morning. He was right when he said I didn't know my way around an engine but I had always wanted to. In the back of my mind, behind all of the other dreams of exotic travel, beautiful women and sports victories sat an innate desire to turn a wrench on an old car.

Growing up I had a neighbor who decided to take me under his wing. Mark Evans. He was already a great grandfather by the time we moved in and got to know the man. His skin was the color of time and his eyes were as old as granite. A lover of Marlboro reds and NASCAR, his garage and driveway were always cluttered with old cars and pieces of engines. I used to love running over to watch him work on a '67 Nova that would later become the first car I would be in to go over a hundred miles an hour.

Mark would say, "Hey ho, J, what do you say? Why don't you grab that socket wrench and hand it over here."

Or, " Hey J why don't I see you out playing with the other kids. Hanging out with a grumpy old man can't be as fun as playing ball." He would say. Knowing that I had struggled with normal boyhood games. Fitting in with kids my own age was never high on my agenda. I wanted to learn, to listen to the stories of a future that awaited me. I wanted out of suburbia from day one. Ironically, in my middle years, I find myself wanting to go back.

Aldon reminded me of Mark. He had the same way about him. A quiet kind of humor and a larger than life personality. Walking behind Aldon I thought of Mark and missed him. He had passed away a couple years before as a satisfied old man. Which is the highest honor any man can achieve. I quietly wondered what Mark would make of all this. This crazy life that Sara and I had found ourselves in. Although confident in the adventure there was a certain sense of shame that came with all of these experiences. How had I allowed us to get in this situation? Sara, who in every way is a more sensible person, had warned me before leaving New York. In those years and even a little in these years, I was always just a little too hard headed to listen. I trusted my inner voice, I knew that the adventure we were on was the right choice. And now it seemed like Sara was emerging as the confident one. It was just hard to have gotten to such a financial state that our whole lives hung on by the generosity of strangers. In a way I think Mark would have approved. He had always promoted the idea of individual experience. I think some of the other more irrational decisions like leaving the car behind on an empty stretch of highway wasn't the best idea. I do think he would have forgiven me for it later though.

Rounding the corner of the front of the house and coming back to the garage, the Mustang sat in the dull light of the cluttered garage. Its perfect contours and rounded hatchback told of many a fast night, in a time long forgotten. The paint job was a classic red and the interior was faded black leather. Her hood was propped open to reveal the scattered guts of an otherwise perfect vehicle. The engine that hung suspended above the carriage was the pride of all American car enthusiasts, the unmistakable V8 engine with its three hundred and twenty horsepower delivering four hundred pounds of torque. This was the kind of engine that got the girl. She never cared for the man driving it. Just for the rumble and the roar and the acceleration of the monster under the hood.

"Alright, alright, stop drooling and come over and help me with the engine." Aldon laughs with a tone of sarcasm but I can tell he's pleased that I love the car like he does.

"She's a beaut, Aldon. A real dream car." I say with wanting.

"Well, she's not for sale, you can't have her." He laughs.

We wrestle with the engine for a moment before perfectly positioning the block above the carriage. It only took a few moments of stress and a few curses before Aldon was able to lower it down into position while I guided the greasy metal chunk into place. A satisfying thud reminded us that it was in its correct slot and we stood back to admire our ten minutes of effort. "Hey grab us a couple beers, what do you say J?" Aldon says with a twinkle. I stop and stare for a moment because it's so much like Mark that I wonder if it's him. But it's not and that's ok, I think. I almost skip to the fridge and grab a couple ice cold PBRs. I toss one over to Aldon from the other side of the car and I'm feeling so comfortable I blurt out, "Hey any chance we can throw on some tunes. Seems kind of perfect for it doesn't it?" I say with a laugh. There's a moment of silence, Aldon's face drops into a frown, I can sense the tension building and then, "Hell yes we should put some music on, smartest thing you've said all day J." He laughs, letting his face bounce into the most joyful happy Santa you've ever seen. He wades through the mess to a massive old sound system and presses a button. In moments the cluttered garage is awash in sixties rock and roll. The beach boys singing "Good Vibrations" brings Aldon to a little dance, both of his hands moving up and down, fists clenched, pursed lips and totally lost in the music. His white beard bobbing and his jolly belly shaking. I laugh and join him in a little dance. We're in full swing now. Laughing and joking back and forth. He asks for a socket wrench and I run over to the bench and search hopelessly through the clutter. He yells at me in his joking tone and I finally toss him the wrong wrench only for him to bend over laughing. We drink our beer and dance and turn a screw or two. The Beach Boys turn into the likes of Jimmy Buffett and The Eagles. We're both singing along to all the songs and having a joyous, old boy time. After about three beers and twenty songs we've got the engine in, connected and ready to be tested.

"Alright James, my boy, this is the moment I've been waiting for. Grab another beer and lets jump in and see if we did it right." He says excitedly, rubbing his hands and grabbing the keys out of his overalls. I grab another red, white and blue and open the doors and jump in. The smell of gasoline and engine oil and leather met my senses and it's one of those perfect smells that stand shoulder to shoulder with the scent of the forest and ocean. For a moment Aldon lingers, key in hand, right next to the ignition. "Cmon baby, start for me this time. Let me hear you purrrrr..." He pops in the key and gives it a jingle and a turn ignites the engine and the whole car starts to vibrate with the power and glory.

"Whooooo"!! Aldon cries out, honking the horn twice and pumping his fist into the air. He opens up the throttle a few times just so we can hear her roar. "Hey, you want to take her out for a ride?" He asks with childlike glee.

"Hell yes I do!" I cry. We stuff our beers into our crotches and fasten our seat belts. He opens the throttle one more time, checks the way is clear and then throws her into gear. We fly to the end of the driveway in a second flat. Checks right, checks left, and then were down the street in a flash of burnt rubber and engine oil. We make our way out onto the coastal highway, wind in our hair and the sound of the engine giving us that special kind of courage. The radio is blasting "Hotel California " and you'll never feel as cool as we did in that cherry red Mustang cruising down the highway as fast as Aldons age would allow. It's a short drive down the coast from the house to the center of the village and we're already passing Henry's shop. Henry, his tall and bent figure, dark with age, is standing outside with a customer when he sees us passing. Aldon honks and throws a middle finger out the window, laughing and gesticulating. Henry shakes his head, smiles and kicks at the air behind us as we fly by. There goes Los Gallitos and the Safeway and then finally the post office where we had stood just days ago, broke, hopeless and lost.

In seconds we are outside the city limits and back on the rugged coastal route. The angry ocean crashing against the sheer cliffs and jagged spaces that hide the dark things, we cruise by like falcons at top speed. The radio plays on and the cool sea air is filling our salty lungs. The car handles the windy road magnificently, turning on a dime and keeping speed. The cherry red shining in the afternoon sun. Soon we were stuck behind a logging truck, piled high with dead trees. Aldon, honks twice and speeds to pass, throwing her into fifth gear and flying past like a bat out of hell. The truck driver looks down at us in annoyance but then appreciation as we drive by. Popping back on the right side of the road we now have the whole coastal highway ahead of us. The steep bluffs to our left lead upward towards the coastal mountain range, occasionally sending small streams trickling down to the sea. The cliff edge to our right plummets straight into the ocean at regular heights of one hundred feet. There is nothing but gentle pastoral land and the two lane highway that winds magnificently ahead of us. Aldon speeds on at eighty miles an hour and laughs and takes occasional swigs of beer. "Ok, what do you say we pop up the 128 and visit a vineyard or two? Well bring the girls back something nice for dinner." Aldon shouts above the roar of the wind and engine. I can barely contain my excitement and just nod and smile and give a thumbs up that says without words, "HELL FUCKING YEAH!!!"

We shortly come to a long and steep hill that runs down from the top of the cliffs all the way to sea level. We gain some momentum but the sheerness of the cliff slows Aldon down as we switch back all the way down to the bottom where a sharp left turn takes us onto Highway 128. The car handles like a champ on the turn and before we know it we're zipping inland and away from the white capped sea. The scenery quickly changes as we follow the Navarro river and enter the last great redwood grove before coming to San Francisco.

Massive, sky scraper sized redwoods that stretch up to the heavens and turn the cars that pass underneath them into tiny little automatons. As this is the only real highway for miles that will take you back inland, it is crowded with slow moving vehicles. It's not important to go any faster than necessary now and Aldon slows to a comfortable pace, with the windows down, taking in the fresh, clean smell of the forest. The temperature noticeably drops while in a redwood forest. The crowns of the trees blot out the sun almost three hundred feet above us. Green, red and dark magenta colors filter through the thick trunks of these prehistoric monsters. Imagine for a moment a tree so big that in some places industrious locals have carved tunnels through them large enough to allow a small car to drive through with ease.

For the communities that are scattered amongst the trees, the redwoods have been a source of income for generations. First with the logging industry and the reckless capitalism of the Gilded Age and then again with the advent of tourism and commuter traffic. Towns compete for who can draw the most attention to various world wonders. The age of route 66 still lives on in many of the towns and hamlets that dot the redwood highway. The crash of the logging industry in the area brought about the kind of poverty that makes people rust from the inside out. These ancient tradesmen had been born into the industry. Generations of loggers descended all the way down from the first of the adventurers and profiteers that invaded the area one hundred and fifty years before. Many once thriving towns would crumble to a heap of old rusty cars, meth heads and lost dreams. Not every town was left to rot, along any highway in the Pacific Northwest you'll find little roadside gems that bring you to that magic place you always hoped for and Highway 128 has all of those magical and tragic locales. The first and best being the tiny hamlet of Navarro.

Chapter 6

Grapes on the Vine

You can blink twice and pass the main strip of Navarro while moving any faster than a crawl and that's just what Aldon did as we whipped around a hairpin turn, paying attention only to the megalithic trees hugging the narrow road. Navarro was once the logging capital of the highway but now it has fallen far from its former glory. The biggest draw for a tourist or motorist would be the Navarro Store. The only gas for at least thirty five miles and frequently some of the most random and fantastic occasions.

Just across from the gas pumps is a small outdoor amphitheater and concert venue carved out of the various debris and clutter of the hovel. There, in that humble space have played some of the finest musicians in the world. Right there in the backyard of some of the mightiest trees on earth, with almost no one knowing of the event, artists like Kris Kristopherson and Johnny Winter have rocked the twinkling night away. Only, the most hardcore of fans and stray locals would ever know of the events planned. But this wasn't the only magic of an otherwise forgotten corner of the world. The magic was in the oddly wonderful folk that inhabit the space. Colorful characters, that, when not in the throws of a meth induced high, are some of the most generous and welcoming people you'll ever come across.

Having just almost missed the turn off to the store Aldon nearly screeched to a crawl in order to make the tight turn without completely flipping over. "Let's grab a quick bite and use the john. Maybe even grab a couple cold ones to keep us going until we hit wine alley." He says while quickly unbuckling and jogging off to the outside porta johns that sit just outside of the store. The store itself is reminiscent of a New England barn. Bright red paint and white trim. The building is connected to a large outdoor seating area and wooden deck. A BBQ and scattered picnic tables greet you as you make your way inside the cozy little store. Tightly clustered groves of young redwood trees are scattered throughout the parking lot and just behind the store is one of those deep and mysterious forests you read about in Scandinavian fairy tales. If you're really lucky you might even hear the mating call of the Navarro people, which is the CLING CLING of horseshoes meeting metal. There under the trees you can see a local or two having a beer or a joint and you can either fall in love or just take in the scene. The sliding glass door of the shop opens with a heavy push and the interior greets me with a friendly one armed man in camouflage. "Hey man, how's it going? What can we do for you? I've got some great tamales in the hot cot!" He says at a hundred miles a minute. His balding head is full of smiles and the whole place reeks of secret magic.

"Hey, tamales sound great and maybe some cold beers." I say with some mirth in my belly. Walking straight to the cooler stacked with domestic and imported beers. Colder than the clay, as they say. Local breweries are also scattered all along the secret coastal highways of California and I'm drawn to one of my favorites, an amber ale from a brewery just up the road in Booneville. Quickly grabbing a six pack and heading to the hot food I see the treasures of the hot cot before me.

Separated by a glass pane and positioned in perfect rows are the true gems of the Navarro store. Wrapped in corn husks and a corn mash called masa are the most tender and delicious stewed meats. Each tamale takes time to make, you can't rush these things. Ancient abuelas bent over for hours to lovingly make each tamale. Not all tamales are the same, just like with any ancient cuisine, regions separate style and ingredients. You're never going to get the same tamale twice. In a tamale the corn is the focus with the stewed meats being the secondary flavor. Growing up in San Diego I knew many wonderful Mexican families who taught me the secret ways of the tamale. "It's all about the corn mijo and never use the banana leaf, only the corn husk." Mireya would say. She was our nanny growing up and we loved her like a mother.

These particular tamales, sitting in perfect form in front of me, were clearly well made. I ordered six of them to share and take home to the girls. They would keep while we had our adventures. Ringing me up at the checkout counter, Dale, the one armed man, chatted amicably. "So are you guys headed up to the coast or out to the vineyards? Great day for it anyway you look at it. If it was me I'd head out to the coast and get some of that sunshine in before we don't see it for about six months." Taking a breath after speaking a hundred words in five seconds he wraps everything up in a brown bag and says, " That'll be fifteen dollars please." I dole out the cash and with a smile and a quick response, " Yeah we're heading out to the vineyards, living on the coast, I'll definitely be back. Thank you!" I say with a flourish and I'm back outside the sliding door again with all the fresh air and excitement. On the deck just outside I see Aldon sitting and smoking with a tall and thin mountain hippy. His scraggly long hair is covered by a knitted beanie accentuated by a colorful outfit that fits his long and skinny frame. His smile goes from ear to ear and two twinkling brown eyes glance up at me as I approach.

"I hear your Aldon's new hired man? You couldn't have found a better guy to work for, I'll tell you that. Call me Green Bean." He says in a serious tone despite his smile. He extends his long arm and his giant hand grasps mine pleasantly. "My name's James, nice to meet ya." I say with a smile. Aldon gestures for me to take a seat. Grabbing the brown bag from me he pulls out the six pack and gives each of us a beer. "Well Jas, you are in the presence of a living legend my friend. This here is the one and only Green Bean. He was one of the original Earth Firsters." Aldon says in a hushed tone.

"Well, it was a long time ago. I'll tell you about it another time." Green Bean says dismissively. For a few seconds there's silence at the table until Aldon cracks open his beer, leans back and gives out a mighty wolf howl that wakes up the entire town.

"You crazy old bastard, scared the hell out of me Aldon." Says a shaken Dale just emerging from the store. Laughter erupts and everyone is shaking Dale's hand again, even me. Sitting down we offer Dale a beer and he gladly accepts. "Hey man, that is one beautiful ride. What is she? A sixty five?" Dale asks. "No, she's a sixty seven. And thanks, we just dropped the engine in her today. Out for a test drive." Aldon says with pride. Green Bean starts to expertly roll a joint and the conversation turns to this year's crop.

"Well, I heard Jim Bridger's indoor got struck with a mean case of spider mites." Or "Yeah and did you hear that Janine Truluck's crop got raided by Mexican gangsters posing as cops?" Times had changed since the Golden Age of the Emerald Triangle, explained Green Bean. This remote region of Mendocino County was once the wild west, where almost no authority cared to venture. Local law enforcement knew most of what was going and would regularly turn a blind eye. It wasn't corruption in any kind of diabolical sense. This was actually a prime example of a caring and service oriented police department. Most of the growers in the area were generational locals. People that had grown up and contributed to society for decades. Times were tough and the sheriff understood that the golden crop of green would be the primary breadwinner for most families. And hey, after all, if you can't afford to pay your taxes you're out of a job anyways. So most people just looked the other way when a farmer was harvesting. Mendocino County was that last bastion of free trade and lawlessness of the west you only read about in old country westerns. But all of that had changed with new drug policies focused on the large marijuana crops of the Pacific Northwest. This region historically supplied almost sixty percent of the entire country's cannabis trade. A multi million dollar, tax free industry operating right under the noses of one of the most tax hungry governments in the entire country. If there was money being made the state of California wanted its piece of the pie. And fair enough. But it changed the mood from community togetherness and friendship to desperation and paranoia. Small growers were getting busted and seeing jail time, not to mention their land being seized by the feds. And the cross over of dangerous gangs taking advantage of cheap land and locals who could keep their mouths shut. Life was still good here, but it was not without its problems.

"We're headed up to the vineyards, going to show J here a few good spots, grab something for the ladies back home." Aldon says.

"Hey man, that's a great idea. If you've never been you should check out Navarro. It's just over the hill and it's one of the oldest vineyards in the valley." Green Bean says in a tone that suggests there can be no other option.

"That's exactly what I was thinking, Green Bean my friend."Aldon exclaims. The joint is lit and my new friends huddle around to finish it off in just a few puffs each. "Alright let's hit the road J. We've got to get back in time for dinner or Sharon will skin me alive." He says while groaning to his feet. We all stand up and shake hands and promise a reunion soon. Grabbing the bag of tamales and remaining beers we jump back into that gorgeous slick, piece of American pie. Aldon honks two times and we're back up the winding road. "Those guys are all crazy, J, good people though." He says with a half smile. The road winds in perfect form through the last of the redwoods that shelter the highway. Soon it's back to scrub grass and low lying hills covered in the warm and inviting shade of the California oak.

With barely enough time to finish our open beers we pass a sign that says, Navarro Vineyards 200 yards to the left. Aldon puts the Mustang into a lower gear and we slow to take the sharp turn in the tucked away parking lot that leads to the vineyard. In that blink of an eye you don't have the time to fully process the beauty of the vineyard itself. You save that for when you finally exit the vehicle and take a moment to breathe it all in.

In the foreground, behind a humble tasting room a massive vineyard stretches out and up onto the distant hills. From the edge of the carpark the vineyard starts and the neat, perfect rows of vines line up to greet us. Each vine is heavy with ripe grapes bursting with sacred juice. In the green space between the vineyards and the tasting room, is a sturdy gazebo covered in blooming wisteria and the perfume of the flowers are intoxicating as we walk past. The tasting room itself is not as impressive as the surrounding countryside and open spaces but it's cozy and approachable. Not like some of the tasting rooms in California where it looks so intimidating that you don't even want to get out of your car unless you've got twenty grand in your back pocket. How wine became as pretentious as it is, eludes me. It is literally a fermented juice to be enjoyed by even the lowest of civilized society.

The door to the tasting room swung open easily to reveal a single room with a U shaped bar and walls stocked thick with available vintages. A friendly gentleman who could have been Aldon's twin, with a full white beard and twinkling eyes greets us both with a smile. "Hey there folks, take a seat anywhere you'd like for a tasting, it's free after all!" He says with a voice that almost sounds like music.

"Don't mind if we do." Aldon says in his corny and awkward dad joke way. Taking our seats closest to the sliding back door with the view that stretches out into the hillside vineyards we settle in for the tasting. "Well, my name's Bill and I've been here at Navarro for thirty years. We're most known for our Gewurztraminer and our old vine Pinot's. What would you guys like to start with?" Bill says with a smile.

"This is James' first visit to Navarro, why don't we just try them all." Aldon says with a laugh. "I like the cut of your jib sir, and welcome young man." He responds with similar dad joke humor and you can tell that the two men were cut from the same cloth. If my respect for Aldon hadn't been so great I may have been bored with their outdated humor and sarcastic responses. But it was hard to be annoyed with either of these men, the kind of good natured personalities that only come with a lifetime of struggle and hardship.

"Let's start with the whites and work our way down, shall we?" He reaches behind the countertop to grab chilled bottles of Chardonnay, Gewurztraminer and a Rosé. "Now, most of the vines you see behind us are of the Gewurztraminer and the Chardonnay. Both have won awards and we love them equally. But if you were to really walk away with one experience, I believe the Gewurztraminer is the more important bottle." Bill says with a sweep of his hand. The afternoon light catches the liquid as it is poured expertly into our glasses. "Now, grab the glass by its base and gently give it a swirl. Now bring it to your nose and inhale deeply. Try and see if there are any familiar smells. Ok, good, now for the fun part. Take a sip and roll it over your tongue, let a little oxygen in. Can you taste the fruits and maybe even a little oak.?" Bill says with a wisdom and ease that come with years of experience. We give the glasses a swirl and a sniff. The setting and exciting personalities accentuate the flavors and smells and in my mind's eye I'm imagining a cornucopia of fruits and old oak trees like the ones guarding the border of the vineyard. "

In moments we are ready for the next pour and reaching for the Gewurztraminer he pauses, as if in reverence for the bottle, finally gently grabbing the bottle and pouring an inch in each of our glasses. "Now, this is a real unique pour to the valley and even California. Gewurztraminer is a grape grown in Western Germany near France and it's one of my favorite white wines." Bill says while also pouring a little for himself in a glass set aside. Bringing the glass to my nose I immediately smell tropical fruits like mango and pineapple but then soon after I smell something softer like lychee fruit or pears. It's all so dynamic and wild that I can actually discern the flavor and scent that I let out, "Wow." Both men laugh at my outburst and Aldon slaps my back and asks, "So, is that your first taste of decent wine." I nod my head. "Yeah I've never tasted anything like that. Most of the time I just go for the cheapest bottle of table wine that I can find." I say with a little naivety. I'm of course thinking about those giant jugs of Sangria you see on the very bottom shelf of any supermarket. Usually just a few dollars for a gallon of wine. Two buck chuck or my personal favorite, a bum jug. One finger through the loop, a couple twists of the arm and she's resting on your shoulder while you gulp the alcoholic grape juice down and then run shrieking down the street with all of your drunken, idiot friends like banshees in the night.

So yeah, I'm new to good wine, I think. As I finish my last sip of the golden liquid. Putting the glass down, Bill immediately rushes to the Rosé. "Now, I do love this Rosé but it's a summer wine and I like you guys, so I have a proposal. Why don't we skip this Rosé and I'll throw in another tasting of one my favorite Pinot Noirs. What do you say? Do you trust me?" Bill asks with perfect salesman pitch.

"With my very life, sir. With my very life." Aldon says with a bow. I just nod eagerly and go with the flow as Bill dances off to the back room for the special bottle. Aldon looks over at me and winks. "This should be good". He says quietly.

Bill emerges from the cellar in a single movement. Almost skipping back to the table he flashes us a dusty bottle of a Pinot Noir that's at least twenty years old according to the label. With a flare he sets the bottle in front of us. "Now this, this is something really interesting. Probably one of our very best years. From what we call, "the deep end". I wanted you to try a really nice Pinot if it's your first time." Bill says with a warm smile.

"That's really nice of you, thank you I'd love to try it." I say. He uncorks the bottle and gives Aldon and I healthy pours. The wine tumbles into our glasses in a flourish of inky, dark red oblivion. Bringing the glass to my nose and becoming immediately overwhelmed with the rich, floral smells meeting my senses. In all of my life I had never smelt anything like it. It was the smell of eternal summer. Of endless warm evenings filled with fireflies, sparkling stars and friends. To this day, many years later I can still remember the profile. Dark fruits, cherry, strawberry and chocolate. The silky texture of the wine gliding over my tongue and caressing my mouth in a way that only a gentle lover knows how. Pinot Noir, how I do love thee. The look on Aldon's face let me know that he was roughly feeling the same way. We must have been lost for a while in appreciation because Bill has to clear his throat loudly to shake us back to earth. "That is probably the best thing I have ever tasted." I say in awe. This time the humor is gone from the room and both men just nod their heads in acknowledgment. The wine is so smooth and easy to drink that it's gone before it ever began and the tasting moves on to other delicious Pinots and even a Zinfandel but nothing can compare to that Deep End Pinot.

"So what's your story guys, are you on a trip to the coast?" Bill asks after our last pour. At this point our cheeks are rosy and my speech is beginning to slur. "Well, we live out on the coast. This young man and his wife are giving us a hand with some chores and I thought I'd take him on a spin up here to grab some wine for dinner tonight." Aldon says, appearing far more sober than I. It must be age, or his wine barrel stomach. "Well, Bill, it's been a pleasure but I think it's time we grabbed some wine to go and head back to the women folk." Aldon says while standing up as if he's only just had a cup of coffee and not three glasses of wine. We will definitely take a bottle of that Pinot Noir and a bottle of the Gewurztraminer too. Anything else J?" Aldon asks. "That sounds just fine." I say in response. I do my best to not look like a jerk and stumble out after saying our goodbyes. I promise Bill that I'll be back with my wife and ramble on about something I'm happy to forget later. Aldon shuffles past me to the car giggling. Time must have screamed by because the mid afternoon glare has now shifted to that soft and perfect light of early evening. I can tell that Aldon is in a hurry to get home as we haven't been in touch with the girls all day. We hop back into the dream machine and back out onto the highway. Dropping into third gear Aldon looks at me with a glowing smile and says, "You see J, that's what moving with the wind looks like. You'll find it too. You just need to pick the direction and the wind will do the rest." He says quietly before picking up speed and flying back down the road towards home. The sun is just now going down over the tall hills but the warmth of the autumnal sun still glows over us as we scream past the Navarro store and back into the twilight forest of giants. I am as happy and content as I have ever been. With a sure feeling of the course of my life going in the right direction and the first true sense of hope in a long while. The car roars off down the winding road sending fallen leaves in gusts of swirls and tornadoes that resettle in the soft green patches that lay at the feet of the giants.

Chapter 7

Al Sur de Mexico

By the time we made it back the moon had risen in the sky and the crickets were singing their song as we bolted down the driveway. The lights were on in every window of the house, the garage door opened and out stepped two angry women, hands on hips with a scowl on their faces.

Aldon looks over at me with a worried face and says quietly, "Alright buddy, we're in the shit now. Lets just keep our heads down and say we are sorry. There's nothing more to be done." With resignation we step from the car to face our certain doom.

"Just what the hell were you thinking? Leaving and not telling us where you were going. You left your phone you big dummy. We thought you had driven off a cliff. Another hour and we were going to call the police." Sharon says sharply at both of us but mostly Aldon.

"I'm sorry babe. We just got caught up in the moment. We ended up going to Navarro and grabbing some wine for dinner tonight." Aldon says sheepishly, staring at his feet.

"You're a crazy old man and I love you. But you are in trouble mister. If we didn't have guests I'd throw you in the doghouse without dinner. We were worried sick. And what's your excuse young man? Didn't you think Sara would be worried?" She says pointing a finger in my direction but still looking at Aldon.

"I am sorry Sharon, it was my fault. I had never been to a winery before and I got caught up talking with the vintner." I say, also looking at my feet as contrite as possible.

I can see Sara with her arms crossed and an amused smile on her face. Even Sharon is smiling now and ready for forgiveness.

"Well, that's ok then. We were just really worried that's all. Now come out back, we have something nice to show you." She says taking Aldon's hand and leading him to the back yard. Aldon looks back and gives me a wink and a thumbs up as Sara and I follow them along the side of the house to the backyard. Before us in the middle of the sprawling lawn that had been mowed and trimmed to perfection was a makeshift gazebo and underneath the picnic tables, pushed together and decorated for a banquet. The rafters and covering of the gazebo are strewn with twinkling fairy lights and hanging flowers. The transformation of the previous days were remarkable. It was a gorgeous evening, with the moon rising and the weather being just warm enough to take off our shoes and walk barefoot in the freshly cut grass.

"Wow, you girls outdid yourselves. The backyard looks beautiful. What's with the lights? Are we having a party?" Aldon says.

"Yes, I thought it would be a fun little thing to do with our new friends here. Sara did all the work anyway, mowed the lawns and strung up the lights. She was a great help today." Sharon said with a whimsical tone in her voice. Looking over at Sara with a soft fondness. "It's nice to have young people back in the house." Her voice now tinged with sadness. She looked away and an awkward moment followed.

Aldon cleared his throat and smiled, "Yeah it's been really nice to have you both. We were getting a little bored and needed a new adventure." He says with a laugh in hopes of changing the subject. "Let's get this party started! J, go back to the car and grab the wine out of the trunk." He says while tossing me the keys.

"Aye Aye Captain" I say with a grin. Aldon looks back and flips me the bird with a smile on his face. Trotting back to the car I trip over the garden hose in excitement. Flying forward and just barely catching myself I hear a giggle. Turning to look I find sweet Sara standing behind me, hands behind her back in a blue and white summer dress and black leggings. Her eyes were full of mischief and torment.

"So, you thought you'd get off that easy huh. Where's my apology." She says with a dead serious look on her perfect oval face. I look at her, startled for a moment and almost worried until her face breaks into a huge grin and she jumps into my arms. "I'm just kidding, I wasn't that worried. Poor Sharon was though. She's really sweet and also kind of sad. But I love her and this place is really great isn't it?" She says in hushed excitement. Our lips pressed together and I held her slender body close. These moments are so rare these days, I think. It almost feels safe, like we can be here and sleep easy. We hold hands and grab the wine out of the trunk of the car. Stopping for a moment to admire the car. Sara looks over at me and says slyly, "Since when did you become a car guy?"

Music wafts through the air as we make our way to the backyard, carrying the wine and the bag of tamales. Aldon is dumping charcoal into the barbecue and Sharon is carrying out various side dishes in crystal bowls and setting them around the table. The girls are chatting about Sharon's grandchildren and Aldon is watching the coals burn, waiting for them to be glowing red before putting on the meat.

"Thanks, Aldon, for a really great day. It's hard to put into words how much I needed it." I say with a sigh, after making my way over to stand by the grill, as men do.

"That's alright pal, I needed a day to have some fun too. And we got a lot done. To be honest, I'm just glad Sharon has Sara helping her out." He says while glancing over at the girls. They're sitting under the gazebo with glasses of wine, lost in a pleasant conversation .

"I didn't tell you this earlier but we lost our daughter. About two years ago Sharon got the call that Amber had been in a car crash with our two grandchildren back east in Ohio. The grandkids escaped without a scratch but Amber didn't make it. We had a troubled relationship and I think Sharon always blamed herself for driving her away." Aldon says quietly and matter of factly. His voice trembled just slightly. He stirs the coals, now glowing red hot and looks up at me, briefly meeting my eyes before turning back to the grill. In that moment the youthful spirit of the day died away and I now saw Aldon as a very old and withered man. His form stooped and ancient, no longer made of steel and sand.

"I'm so sorry, Aldon. I can't even imagine what that must be like." I say quietly. In these moments it's impossible to know the right thing to say.

"It just is what it is. Look here, in a moment everything can change. You've got to find the small, magic moments, son. That's all that matters. At this point in my life I laugh at all of the stresses that Sharon and I went through in our forty five year marriage. It's not about the material, it's about the spiritual and the connections you make with people. You and Sara are on the right path. I know it doesn't feel like it with your situation but just remember all of these small moments. Make the best choice you can with the information you have and if it's the wrong move then you step back and try again. There is no right answer, no perfect decision can be made. It's important to remember that being an adult means that you have to make hard decisions and also that no one else is coming to save you" He says.

"Aldon, I've felt lost these last few months. With everything that's happened it just feels like I keep making the wrong move. And now it's too cold to go north. After we leave here I have no idea where we'll go." I say nervously.

"Well, if you can't go north. Why not go south?" He says with a laugh.

He leaves me with that thought and a slap on the back as he goes inside to fetch the meat for the grill. Looking back at the girls I notice them sitting quietly and watching me.

"You know, that's not a bad idea James. You guys can stay here as long as you'd like but I know you're eager to get on the road. You both have that look. Your adventure isn't over yet. The south will be warmer. You said you're from San Diego. Maybe you can visit some family down there?" Sharon says in a motherly tone.

"Heck, screw San Diego. Why don't you guys go to Mexico? Remember that month we spent in Baja, Sharon? One of the best experiences of our life." Aldon says while returning with a platter stacked high with thick cut steaks.

"That's an interesting idea. What do you think babe? Mexico could be fun. Plus it's cheap and will be warmer than here." I say to Sara who is quietly sitting and taking it all in.

All eyes turn to her and she blushes from the sudden attention. Sara hates being put on the spot but something spurs her on to comment excitedly. "Umm yes. That sounds amazing. I don't know why we didn't think of it before?" She says while taking a sip of wine.

I felt a surge of electricity dance in my belly and in that moment I knew we would be heading south. Aldon carefully placed each steak on the grill with a sizzle. The meat is cooking over the coals and the wine in hand. The soft evening air wafting the smells through the neighborhood. For a moment there's silence as we all comprehend this new plan.

"Well, it looks like you have your answer Jim, you are headed to Me-xi-co!" He says with a southern drawl and a loud hoot that echoes off the tall trees in the distance.

From there the night turns into a celebration and any sadness has left both of our hosts. The steak sizzles and is soon served onto paper plates piled high with mashed potatoes and greens. The wine is flowing now and the old buzz from earlier returns as we all lift our full cups to the sky and toast to adventure, the promise of tomorrow and MEXICO!

Chapter 8

Our New Home

Days turned into weeks, holidays came and passed and before we knew it the ambulance had been purchased and the work finished. Each day with Aldon and Sharon had helped to restore our faith in both our journey and humanity. Sara helped to clean and tidy the house, managed the garden and organized Sharon's papers. I spent most of my time with Aldon. We cleaned and rearranged the garage and harvested his marijuana plants. The seasons were changing again and the call to the road was fierce. You could tell that the work was done and that they were being kind by finding small chores to continue to keep us and pay us.

Then the day came when Aldon and Sharon knocked on the van door in the late afternoon to say their goodbyes.

"I think you're ready my friends. The road is calling and it's best you don't keep her waiting much longer. We've loved having you guys and the Ambulance is officially yours. We also wanted to give you this for all your hard work." Aldon said with a sheepish smile. His arm around Sharon and the two of them looking like proud parents sending their young ones off to college. He handed me the title to the ambulance and an overstuffed envelope nearly bursting with money.

"Aldon, that's too much. You guys have been cooking for us and I'd feel bad taking that much." I say, embarrassed by the amount.

"Not a word of it. You've earned every dime. The guys came by and picked up the harvest. We made a tidy sum and this is what we'd pay anyone for the work you've done." He says in a matter of fact tone.

"Please be careful, both of you. And make sure to write to us when you get to Mexico. We'd love to stay in touch and if you ever need anything or are back up this way again, you know you have a place to stay." Sharon says, holding back tears. She gives us each a big hug.

"We're not fond of saying goodbye, it's always, I'll see you later. And remember what I said about the magic. Find it and you'll find exactly what you're looking for. And don't forget about the wind. If you're not traveling with it, you're against it." He says with a smile. They both give us one last wave before quickly heading back to the house.

Now it's just the two of us again alone with an envelope of money and the title to our new home. We look at each other grinning like hyenas.

"How much is in the envelope". She asks excitedly

I tear open the letter and start to count fifties and hundred dollar bills out into neat stacks. The two of us huddled, reveling in our newly earned riches. "Uh, it's over six thousand dollars." I say with shaky hands. We sit for a moment in shock and then together we start to cheer loud enough that I'm sure Aldon and Sharon could hear.

"You see, I told you we should call him. Imagine where we'd be if we had just returned to the beach with those hippies." Sara said, laughing and happier than I've seen her in months.

The excitement was palpable. We had, for the last several days, been making plans with Aldon for Mexico but before that we would stop in a few places along the coast and a quick visit in San Diego before crossing the border. We would head for La Paz at the very southern end of Baja and our map was neatly marked by Sharon, right down to the last mile. The trip was booked and we were ready to go. It was understood that we were welcome to spend the night and leave in the morning at our leisure but the adrenaline was pumping and with only a couple hours of sleep we decided to pull up anchor and set off around three in the morning well before the first light of dawn. As we were pulling away we noticed the front room still had its light on and as we turned on to the road Aldon appeared in the window with one last wave.

There were no cars on the road this early in the morning and we drove at a steady pace through town. The chill, early morning air was kept at bay with our heater roaring and filling the cavernous van with a comfortable presence. Sara was in the back rummaging about, trying to hold on as I took my time on the hair pin turns that lined the coast after leaving Mendocino. Passing Henry's auto shop I gave one last beep of my horn to an empty building. A tribute to a kind hearted man that over the last couple of weeks had stopped by several times to speak with Aldon and to lend a hand turning the van into a livable space. He had built a camper van the previous year and seemed eager to help out on another project.

The van, or ambulance, had an extended roof which allowed for easy movement without having to stoop over. It had already been stripped down to the bare necessities with Aldon who used it mostly to transport gardening supplies and soil. We swept it out and scrubbed it from top to bottom before laying down a comfortable and cheap, blue shag carpet that Henry had left over from his van the year before. The walls of the van were also covered in hundreds of squares of sample carpet sheets that we found in a rubbish bin behind the local hardware store. It was a mishmash of ten different colors that went from floor to ceiling. The front had two seats separated by a large open space where we installed a small, foldable table. The dash had been ancient and dusty when we found it. Soon we had installed a brand new sound system and cleaned all of the cobwebs and dust from her shoulders. Both seats had a lever you pulled and they would swivel a hundred and eighty degrees to face the living area. Plush and comfortable chairs after we vacuumed and shampooed the upholstery made for a relaxing driving space. Under the overhead cabinet a CB radio was attached and dangled just above the driver's head. And for the main attraction, inside of the cabinet was a switch box that operated the two red emergency lights that were set apart on each corner of the front of the ambulance.

"Look, I can't tell you what to do, but if I were you I would not turn those lights on unless you're parked and at a campground somewhere." Aldon had said the day after we rewired the radio and the lights. Big trouble to be had if you get caught doing something like that. The horns that had once belted out the siren were long since rusted and broken and instead of replacing them we just removed them altogether. We liked to travel under the radar, not over it.

In the living space of the ambulance, which took up two thirds of the entire length and area of the vehicle, we decided to install a sizable wall shelf that ran from the front seats to about midway where they dipped down to form a small kitchen and table top. The shelves were lovingly installed by Aldon and I who over the course of a weekend had built them in his garage while drinking beers and listening to country western music. It's a miracle we managed to get them flush and balanced. They were oak and had been felled, dried, cured and cut to precision from a tree that had fallen in the backyard a couple winter storms back. Aldon had taken a furniture making course at the Krenov institute the year before and had lots of leftover material from projects that he had finished. It was a pleasure to watch true craftsmanship at work. His gnarled hands delicately holding the perfectly shaped wood. Using a mallet and chisel he showed me how to make the coveted dove-tail joint that would lock the shelves into place.

Once the shelves had been installed we moved on to the bed. Using two by fours we built a raised bed, with a storage area underneath. The area was large enough for a queen sized bed, allowing my six foot frame to easily stretch out without my feet hanging over the edge. We put down plywood sheets to cover the frame and then Sharon had given us a spare mattress they had been meaning to replace. The day before we left Sharon had taken Sara to get sheets and surprised us with a gift of light blue Egyptian cotton sheets and a cozy, black comforter. So the bed was raised and allowed for a metric ton of storage that would quickly be filled with useful items like an old cook stove that Aldon didn't want anymore and a portable tire pump that also could jump your battery if need be. He also gave me his son's old seven foot long surfboard that just barely fit but would come in handy in Mexico. I was most excited about this. Growing up in San Diego I had learned how to surf early and missed the gentle pleasure of waiting for a wave. We stuffed our full backpacks underneath and still had room for more. Directly behind the bed were the two big double doors that opened outwards. We left a space for a small circular table and shelf that held a mini bar and an antique globe we found in the basement that no one wanted.

We solved the problem of lighting by stringing up about fifty feet of battery operated fairy lights that we wrapped around the rim of the inside. When turned on, the whole living area was transformed into a cozy and magical space.

From the bed to the front cab was about five feet of open space that we could both sit cross legged in. The shag carpet felt perfectly delicious underfoot. A fold up table and a small charcoal BBQ were also squeezed in next to a full sized igloo cooler that Sharon had made sure to stock with hot dogs, buns and various perishable snacks for our first couple nights on the road. It was a good start to making the ambulance a livable and comfortable space.

"Hey can you slow down please, I'm trying to find the tape deck adapter thingy." She said, annoyed with how fast I was taking a turn.

"I honestly can't go any slower, these are crazy turns." I say while white knuckling it around yet another hard turn.

"Well can we pull over for a second somewhere? I want to get our music set up and reorganize for a minute."

"Yeah there's a spot coming up it looks like." I say while squinting in the early morning darkness. Approaching a pull off that led to a small parking lot perched on a cliff side trail I turned off the road and backed into a parking space with the rear of the ambulance facing the inky darkness of the ocean. I popped the clutch into park and turned off the van. The excitement of the morning still hasn't left either of us and I swivel my chair around to face Sara.

"Ok thanks, I'm going to turn on the fairy lights so I can see what I'm doing." She says with enthusiasm.

"I still can't believe we have this. It's so cozy. I can't wait for tonight. I don't even care how far we go today. As long as we find the perfect campsite near the ocean and maybe some vineyards." I say, rambling to Sara's back while she rummages around under the bed looking for the adapter.

"I can't hear what you're saying, I know I put this stupid adapter somewhere." She says in a muffled tone hinted with annoyance.

"Found it! I knew it was here." She says with a smile as she emerges from under the bed holding up the tape adapter.

"I said, I'm super excited to be on the road in our new and cozy home. What if we just drive however long we want today? We don't need to push it. I'd love to stop near a coastal vineyard or a quiet place near the ocean." I say quickly. Sara's patience is short for small talk but I just can't contain my excitement.

"I think that's a good idea. I'm not in a rush. Where are we now? Did we even make it twenty miles down the road?" She said smiling.

"Ha, yes, we're about thirty five miles south of the turn that heads towards Navarro. This is the real lost coast, I think. Next town is Point Arena and then Bodega Bay before we get to San Francisco." I say.

"I'd like to make it through San Francisco if we can. Would be nice to be on that stretch of the highway before we stop. Maybe we can spend the night in Santa Cruz?" She asks quietly.

"Yeah that's perfect. Should be about six hours."

"We're missing something."

"What?"

"She needs a name."

"What are you thinking?" I ask.

"I dunno, something historic and grand." She says.

"What about, the Endeavor? After the famous ship."

"We can call her Andy for short!" She laughs

"I like it, Ok, so you grabbed the adapter? Should we get this show on the road?" I say, eager to get a move on. If we can make the Golden Gate bridge before too long we can avoid the crazy traffic of the city.

She jumps into the front seat and I swivel my chair back around to the front, locking it into place. She injects the adapter into the tape deck and connects it to our iPod and starts scrolling through the music. The horizon has that early morning glow to it, just now showing itself as the sun kisses the other side of the ocean one last time before emerging to light up the world.

Pulling out of the car park and accelerating south at reasonable speeds while the radio blasts,

On the road again, like a band of gypsies
We go down the highway
Were the best of friends
Insisting that the world be turning our way…..

Chapter 9

The City by the Bay

The midday sparkle of sunshine poured through the window of the Endeavor as we arrived in Bodega Bay. For the last several hours we had slowly trickled our way down Highway 1, ignoring some of the smaller little villages along the way, we promised to stop in Bodega for the seafood market and a snack.

The coast prior to arriving in Bodega is an amalgamation of the sweetest dreams. A peaceful, two lane highway on some of the most dramatic coastal lands in the world. No one is here, I think, as we drive in the pattern of a slithering snake. Tight hairpin turns let out onto gorgeous, empty highways with the sea on your right and the coastal plains to your left. On occasion you're met with mountains and towering hills but it's short lived as the sea takes all the attention.

Shortly after a long stretch of nothing but the sea and the hills we see a nondescript green highway sign that simply says, *Bodega Bay, Pop 950, Elevation 45.*

"We're here!" She exclaims victoriously.

"Yeah, now let's try and find that seafood market. I remember it being somewhere on the right." I say while squinting in the light.

"There it is, just up ahead on your right. I can see the sign." She says.

"Awesome. I'm hungry. Maybe we can get something to put in the cooler to cook up later on the fire." I say with a grumble in my stomach. We had skipped breakfast with all of the adrenaline pumping on our departure. My stomach had been making noises for the last twenty miles or so of hair pin turns. That coupled with the salt air and the cool morning made me as hungry as a starving sailor.

The Bodega Bay seafood market is part of a larger tourist attraction with stores and sweet shops attached. With the hordes of travelers coming from San Francisco, just about every business caters to the whims of tourism. Bodega Bay is a colorful little fishing village that looks trapped in the 1950s. The market advertises everything from fresh caught salmon, halibut and tuna to oysters, mussels and various other specimens of the sea.

Parking the van in the crowded lot was difficult but we finally managed to squeeze into a space closest to the road. Our giant marshmallow of a vehicle looked awkward next to all of the sedans and smaller cars. The space was so tight that we had to climb out the back to avoid opening our door onto a brand new BMW.

The fresh sea air whooshed into the van as we swung open the back doors, garnishing attention from several curious onlookers. Stepping down and out into the parking lot brought another wave of excitement. Here we were, finally, back on the road and having a true adventure. Having earned enough to resume our voyage it was easy to want to spend. We were free to do what we wanted and there is no freedom quite like the open road and a spending spree at a local fish market.

The electronic doors opened soundlessly as we stepped up to the building. Inside were row after row of raised beds, filled with crushed ice and layered with fish. At the very front you had whole salmon laid out in neat stacks. Tuna, and halibut in the next bed. Smoked fish and crabs in the next. The rest of the store was filled with expensive trinkets, hot sauce, local fudge wrapped in cellophane and over priced shirts and hoodies. We wandered in and slowly took it all in.

Gravitating to the middle rack full of oysters, mussels and smoked fish we found ourselves pulled into a sales pitch by an employee. He is tall and gangly with the kind of arrogant swagger that screams of small town shenanigans and disgruntled locals. The corners of his lips are stained yellow from smoke and an invincible stubble rests on his chin. His arms wave wildly while showing us the fish bed.

"Hey guys, we just got these giant oysters fresh. We harvest them right in the bay. Also check out our smoked salmon. I'll give you one guess where we smoke them?" He says with a smirk.

"Uh, here?" I say, willing to go along with the joke.

"Nope, we get it from Stinson Beach further south." He laughs.

"You got me, any chance we can grab some ice to pack in our cooler. I definitely want to get a dozen oysters and some smoked salmon." I say. The fishmonger is entertaining but his brash personality has penetrated into our magical private world and I can tell that Sara wants to find what we're looking for quickly and get back to the safety of our van.

"No problem at all. I'll get that wrapped up for ya now." He says and in less than a minute were paid and on our way out. His smirk could be felt burning into our backs as we turned to leave. We had purchased about a pound of smoked salmon. That with the cream cheese and crackers we had stored away in the cooler would make the perfect mid day snack. We would have spent more time but on first glance everything was far more expensive than we had expected. We could find better things cheaper further south, we thought.

The BMW had gone, leaving plenty of room for us to slide open the side door to pack up the cooler full of oysters and the crushed ice. Looking back inside the van we were pleased to find that the drive hadn't dislodged any of the wall carpet or the shelves. The cabin looked as snug as a bug in a rug. We climbed in and shut the door behind us, closing off the rest of the world and sealing us back into our ship of the imagination. The plush feel of the shag carpet curled around our toes as we sat and quickly ate the smoked salmon and cream cheese. Each sweet and smokey bite revitalizes us. We're in a hurry to get through San Francisco though and the road is calling so we hop back up into the front and strap in. The van rumbles to life and before we know it we're winding past Bodega Bay and further towards Stinson Beach.

Stinson Beach is one of those perfect, secret beach communities that can suck you in and keep you forever. If you're not careful, like Navarro, you can miss the town if you're going too fast. With just a few shops and restaurants on the highway the rest of the town slips into the hills and down by the sea that's covered in a pleasant forest of beech trees and bush. But we are not ready to be stolen by Stinson just yet. That would come in later years. For now our mission was set on getting through San Francisco. Now that it's early afternoon the road is starting to fill up with motorists headed to Stinson and Bodega and before we know it we're turning onto Highway 101 and merging into midday traffic.

What a shock. To leave the peaceful meanderings of the coastal highway, thrust into the frantic driving of hundreds of disgruntled city folk. Traffic is hated universally. If you know of someone who loves traffic you should call the police. They most likely have bodies under the floorboards. Traffic is diabolical. One of modern life's true and unnecessary tortures. Everyone is in a rush to get nowhere. The shorter your distance, the faster and more dangerously you drive. It always amazes me to witness the attitudes of city drivers. It's as if they've lost the will to live or that they mistakenly believe that health care is free. It is a dog eat dog world where the victor takes the spoils. You must be aggressive or you will be taken by the tide and stuck forever in purgatory.

Driving aggressively in a giant marshmallow is only doable theoretically. Practically it will likely give your wife a heart attack. The massive engine in the van is roaring as I try to accelerate past a merging tractor trailer and behind him is an angry corvette, buzzing like a bee looking for a chance to steal his way past everyone.

"Please, can you slow down? This is terrifying." She says meekly as the angry bee drives past honking and weaving in and out of traffic.

"I'm trying but there's not much I can do." I say angrily. Staring daggers into the backs of all the passing cars I weave in and out, adjusting to the flow and doing my best to not lose control.

Finally the traffic settles to a steady flow as we near the first of the tunnels leading us to the bridge. Entering the great opening of the first we instinctively suck in air to hold our breaths. We've had this tradition from our very first road trip years earlier and I've often wondered if anyone else has it? Do you? Do you hold your breath whenever you enter a long tunnel, for good luck or to ward off the evil spirits. We make a wish, what do you do?

We plunge out into the light and quickly approach the second tunnel, this one just slightly longer and much harder to hold our breaths as we near the exit. In a moment we breathe in and then, with wide eyes take in the view of the great and glorious Golden Gate bridge. Its two monolithic structures, gleaming red against the deep blue of the sea and verdant green and gray of the city and of the headlands behind it, draping her arms from one side of the bay to the other.

The giant marshmallow van plummets towards the entrance of the bridge, keeping pace with the other savage contestants. The sun is shining and the brilliant colors of the bridge and bay welcome us as rubber touches metal and concrete.

"Roll down your windows! I want to feel the wind of the bay!" I shout while cranking the window down and thrusting my head out, keeping one hand on the wheel and howling like a wolf in the silhouette of a full moon. She rolls down her window sending her hair flying while the radio blasts songs of freedom and the rust colored monolith welcomes us as we pass under the first tower. Looking quickly and nervously to the right we see the great expanse of the Pacific Ocean and to the left the city, perched in cluttered order like a great shining city on a hill. It's all there, we think. The world and whatever else is beyond that. There is magic in this air, I think.

"Roll up the windows, I'm getting chilly." The woman says as we approach the toll booths with big flashing neon signs that say to SLOW DOWN!

"Alright, alright. I love the wind in my face. Can you see it? It's beautiful!" I say while waving my arms in the direction of the bay.

"Yes, yes. I see it. Please pay attention to the road. How much is this going to cost?" She says, pulling me back to earth and my attention towards the approaching toll booth.

"It says five dollars. Grab my wallet." I say while pulling up to the man in the box.

She hands me five one dollar bills and I press them into the man's hands. He looks tired and unimpressed with our beautiful new home or my generous smile. He flicks a switch and the barrier lifts and we are free to enter the city and all of its shining glory.

Chapter 10

Chinatown

The small, waterside district of Fort Mason has been asleep since 1955. Having been an established military post from the Civil War on, it escaped most of the cultural revolutions of the mid twentieth century. Snug against the Golden Gate bridge and stretching all the way to Fisherman's Wharf it is a quiet respite in a sometimes hectic city.

San Francisco is a lot like a Miles Davis album. You have the lonely aching horn and the tapping drums. The funky bass line and an experimental instrument coming together to make something beautiful and previously unseen by humankind.

Coming down the 101 we decided on a whim to veer left on Marina blvd to head towards the hills of Fort Mason, where we could be sneaky and park our car in the lot of an old hostel who rarely saw a parking attendant. Coming past the park on the left we turn into the National Parks Conservancy and wheedle our way through the buildings to a hidden away parking lot close to Bay st. We've always been safe here on previous trips. Once, when on our way back from a failed trip to Hawaii we huddled in the shelter of the Conservancy with nothing but the clothes on our backs and the warmth of each other. It was a rough night but the area was now fixated in our lexicon of favorite places. Sometimes the roughest moments give us our fondest memories.

"Ok this is a good spot. We can park here and just wander about for a couple hours." I say.

"I don't want to stay too long but I'm still hungry. Let's get something to eat as well." She says with urgency.

"It's already two o'clock, maybe we should think about just staying here in the city tonight. Get an early start for Santa Cruz in the morning." I say, because I can feel the pulse of the city pumping through my veins. The smell, the sounds, the sights. She looks at me with annoyance but can tell I've already made up my mind.

She jumps into the back to rummage about for her wrap while I put on my thick, black hoodie. The air is cool and wet as we lock the van and stroll towards the hostel and the wharf. We hold hands and walk past the corner where we had spent a restless night. Glancing only quickly, the memory was a bitter one and there was no reason to ruin our buzz.

"Whatever we do, we need to remember to replace the ice in the Igloo. I want those oysters tomorrow in Santa Cruz." She says, coming to terms with the spontaneity of the moment. Giant eucalyptus trees line the walkway as we pass the hostel and make our way down the steep hill towards the bay with the swimmers. Even now, in the beginning of winter they are wading into the ice cold sea in speedos and onesies. I think about the levels of discipline it must take to get them into the water. A discipline I will never have, I say to myself as we pass them by. The crowds are starting to become apparent as we find ourselves on the Embarcadero near Fisherman's wharf with all of the colorful shops and restaurants. On the corner of Jefferson and Mason is the Madame Tussauds wax museum. Overpriced wax statues of famous people I don't care about. Continuing on towards Pier 39 the crowds have reached a fever pitch. I can tell that the woman is getting frustrated and on the verge of hating the moment so I pull her away and we turn south on Stockton street to head towards our very favorite part of the city. Chinatown.

San Francisco is completely walkable. From North to south and East to West you can find a sure path that will carry you to your destination. From the Embarcadero to Columbus street is maybe a twenty minute walk and far less stressful than the swarm of humans gathering in great cluster fucks at the Pier. Our pace quickens with excitement as we get closer to our favorite places. Quickly passing little Italy and finally turning left on Columbus to make our way to the Vesuvio Cafe.

The Vesuvio has been a haunt of beatniks, hippies, punk rockers and poets for generations. A thousand creative souls had passed through over the years and some still lingered in its former glories. The facade of the building is painted in adventurous colors while an alley that separates it from the famous City Lights bookstore has a story written in paint and poetry. Coming up to the small door in the front and the sign says CLOSED until 3pm.

"Shoot, I wanted to get a snack and a drink here." She says with disappointment.

"That's ok, let's just wander into Chinatown and find something to eat. Even something small." I say.

"Oooh I want dumplings." She says with renewed enthusiasm. Grabbing my hand she pulls me eagerly down the alley and towards the back way into the district. Her features are on fire today, I think. Her gorgeous dark hair in perfect curls bouncing and guiding me. She is in her favorite brown shawl that hangs loosely around her narrow shoulders and petite figure. Looking back at me her eyes are full of mischief and fun. The stress of traffic has officially melted away and she's ready for fun.

Leaving the alley and turning left on Grant we enter into a new kind of clutter. This feels more authentic and less stressed out. Every business and face belongs to an oriental design. We're skipping past Mings market where the plucked chickens hang behind a plexiglass window and then onto Lee's Market with the scattered wooden crates filled with fruits and exotic vegetables. Hanging from building to building are banners written in mysterious Chinese script and the crowds push us onwards like a great current. We're getting hungrier now as we pass by restaurants spewing their enticing smells in great tendrils of smoke and steam that meet our senses with almost every step. It's sweet and savory and can only be found in places like this.

"I'm so hungry now, I honestly would go to any of these places." I say impatiently. Darting glances in every restaurant's entrance looking for a sign to lead me in the right way.

"No way, we have to go to Sam Wo's. It's tradition." She says with confidence. "How can you even consider anything else?" She continues.

"I don't know, I just wasn't in the mood for that grumpy waiter. But now that we're saying it out loud I don't know how I could consider anything else." I laugh and pick up the pace.

Sam Wo's is an institution so established that when it was closed for health and safety, a crowd of angry picketers waved signs and chanted into bullhorns until the city let it reopen. Its nondescript neon sign guides you into what can only be described as a lazy man's city shack. Its jagged door is as unfriendly as the host who greets you in a small entrance after swinging open the door. Usually the host will just motion for you to follow him, through the busy kitchen with hanging poultry and an angry chain smoking chef, is a small set of wooden stairs that lead you to the second floor. In a cramped space with only a handful of tables and a dumbwaiter you can order some of the finest Chinese food in the city. It is always full of grease and MSG and possibly salmonella and rickets and all of the other bacterias that are spread by unsanitary methods. But it is excellent. Or was. Now its moved locations after the city condemned the building and it just never was the same after the original, crotchety owner had died.

"What do you want?" The sweaty, slightly balding man asks unkindly in a thick accent.

"I want the pork dumplings please."

"I'll take the seafood chow mein." I say while pointing to the menu that's laminated onto the table.

"Anything to drink?" He asks in a hurry.

"Two beers please." I say with confidence.

The server grunts, and turns around to trot down the stairs and can be heard yelling directions at the angry chef. The sound of a commotion, banging pots and pans and I swear I heard a chicken SQUAWK.

"God, I love this place. It never changes." I say as the angry waiter arrives with two mugs of ice cold beers. We immediately gulp them down, out of thirst and also adrenaline and hunger.

"Two more beers, please." I ask the waiter as he's on his way past us having just taken the order of the only other couple there. They look confused and we figure it's their first time. Be patient, my friends, I think. The food will speak for itself.

"Already more beers. I don't want no funny stuff tonight please." The waiter says with words dripping with venom and returns to the kitchen to shout even louder at the chef or the chickens or whoever might be in his way. We exchanged glances with the couple seated next to us and we all burst into laughter.

What seems like an eternity passes before a bell dings and the waiter arrives to slide open the dumbwaiter where a tray filled with delicious food appears. With contempt he slams our beers down and begins to deliver our food. A steaming, round bamboo basket stuffed with perfectly made dumplings and a heaping plate of greasy noodles with chunks of seafood and mystery meat. The food had barely left the dumbwaiter before we slurped it down and stuffed it into our faces. Each salty, sweet bite washed down with a swig of ice cold Chinese beer. The room is starting to heat up with the food and the small crowd and the windows are fogging over bringing the outside light, full of neon and splendor dancing through the room.

The ratio of how long it takes to eat your food versus how long it takes to get your food is grossly unbalanced. Once that first savory bite is finished the race is on. Chopsticks move at lightning speeds, capturing dumplings and noodles and shrimp. Nothing is spared, nothing is safe. The beer disappears before the meal and just as if it all were a dream, we get up and shuffle down the stairs and out the rickety door waving goodbye to the angry chef and the disgruntled waiter who, sitting on a stool at the foot of the stairs just shrugs and looks away. Our mission complete, the food is settled and we're back on our way into the glittering night.

"Let's go back to Vesuvio, it's open and I want a stiff drink." I say, moving into a confident stride back down Grant towards the alley. I can feel the electricity of magic tonight. You've had the feeling to. Where the energy of the night flows in your veins, enough to make your hair stand up. The cool early evening air is brisk enough to add to the excitement and we quicken our steps.

"So we're definitely staying in the city tonight." She says with a hint of sarcasm.

"I just want the night to take us. I don't want to make plans. I feel like something special is happening, don't you?"

"Ok, ok. I want to feel the magic too. I guess we can have some fun." She says with a resigned smile.

We link arms and walk under the neon lights and smile and think about how these are the small moments that Aldon had mentioned. Looking around at the adventure before us I did my best to soak in the moment. To look down at my beautiful wife with her dark curls billowing in the small breeze. Her perfect mediterranean features are accentuated by the colorful night and we can both feel the cosmic rush of possibility.

The Vesuvio is all lit up and the stained glass windows glow and beckon us to enter. The wooden doors open to a long bar that runs the length of the room with small snugs and tables tucked away at the front and side. A second story balcony wraps around the sides of the building creating an open space for spectators to enjoy the early years of the Beat poetry scene. Here in these hallowed halls Jack Kerouac read lines of verse and Allen Ginsberg reciting *Howl*. Everything is made of old, well worn wood and it has the same cozy effect that an ancient English country pub would have.

It's not very crowded. A spattering of tables are taken up by locals and tourists alike. The bar only has one older gentleman, perched in the corner seat of the bar hunched over a glass of wine. A slender dark haired girl is behind the bar facing away from us as we come up and pull out stools to sit on a few seats away from the huddled man.

The old man looks over at us and gives a cough to alert the bartender. She spins around and her pearlescent oval face is set under a perfect fringe and long black eye lashes. She moves gracefully to us and looks straight into my eyes for a long pause and then asks.

"Hey, what can I get you?" She asks, turning directly to Sara.

"Two Hemingways please." Sara says, meeting her gaze.

"Wow, fancy. Where are you guys from?" She asks, turning to grab the Absinthe and Champagne, setting the bottles in front of us and pausing.

"New York, we're on an epic odyssey of sorts." I say with awkward enthusiasm.

She looks over at Sara and with a sarcastic grin says, "An odyssey huh, does he always talk like this?"

"Ha, yes it gets worse the more he drinks," Sara says laughing.

"Well, let's get him good and sauced then shall we?" She says with a wicked grin. Grabbing two Champagne flutes she first pours a healthy shot of Absinthe and then tops the glass off with Champagne. She sets both glasses down in front of us and sets off to help a new customer. We each delicately take hold of our potent cocktails and leave the bar behind to climb the wooden steps and find a seat with a view. Passing our bartender on the way up, she looks up at both of us and gives us a flirtatious wink.

We look at each other and giggle as we find a snug to squeeze into next to a window that looks out onto the street. We can see all of the wastrels and wanderers as they pass by below, unsuspecting of watchful eyes. The hard wooden benches have old throw pillows and we sit across from each other before taking a long, delicious sip.

"That girl was totally flirting with us right?" Asks Sara in a hushed tone. She has a smile from ear to ear and her cheeks are full of blush and excitement.

"See, I told you there was magic in the air." I say with a laugh and a cheeky grin. She laughs and squirms a bit on her cushion.

"She looks like someone we know, or maybe want to know. I can't place it but she reminds me of someone and I kind of think it's hot. Is that weird?" She says, in a hushed fluster.

I laugh because it's all so obvious, you can never tell you're looking in the mirror until your image smiles back. The bartender and Sara could be cousins. Both with their alternative style and dark hair.

"You guys look exactly alike, can't you see it?" I say laughing.

"No way. Do you really think so? She's taller and has a different haircut." She says nervously while toying with her perfect curls.

"I don't know, there's just something about her that reminds me of you." I say while taking another healthy sip of the cocktail. I can already feel the absinthe soaking into my liver and it's making my cheeks feel warm and my lips are fixed into a permanent smile.

"Well don't look so pleased with yourself."

"I'm not, how dare you assume..."

"I would do it, by the way."

"You would?"

"Yeah, why not. We're on an adventure right?"

From those delicious words the next couple hours scream by. A different waitress comes and takes our order for another round, and then another but this time wine. Red wine. Deep, burgundy in color and French in name. A group of people come and sit next to us. They are philosophy students at Berkeley and came for a pint and to revel in the history. Soon enough our conversations end up crossing over and we push our tables together to form one long and loud gathering. The talk is about Kierkegaard and existentialism. It's a lot of fluff and pomp, with no one really making any points outside of who likes to hear their own voice more. Myself included. I'm getting bored and can tell that Sara is ready to be back in our world so we excuse ourselves and make our way back down stairs towards the bar and the exotic doppelgänger slinging drinks.

"Hey guys, did you finally get bored of those wind bags?"The bartender says with her sarcastic laugh. She moves to make us another round but I hiccup and say,

"I think we might just head off actually, we wanted to get your name though. Maybe we'll see you again somewhere down the trail."

"What! No, don't leave. I'm off in like half an hour. Do you guys want to get a drink somewhere? I need to hear about this odyssey." She pleads and locks eyes with both of us.

Sara and I look at each other and shrug. Excited for whatever might happen and settle into the two stools near the old man, who is still perched in his corner. He lifts a grumpy eye to us and snorts.

"Yeah sure, why not." I say smiling. She prances up to the shelf with the wine and uncorks an older looking bottle. Coming back she flashes another flirtatious grin and pours us each a glass.

"This ones on me and I'll be off in just a bit." She says while rushing off to help another group of thirsty patrons. We sneak a quick, secret glance and turn to our wine and to look around at the bar. It's almost completely packed at this hour and the drinks are flying out of the bar just as fast as our new friend can make them. Her dark, straight hair occasionally falls in her face while she shakes and stirs and pours.

"That one is a wild cat." Says the old man suddenly while looking directly at us with both eyes now. On closer inspection he's a curious fellow. Wearing a mole skin trench coat, a woolen scarf and a trilby hat that's pushed back on a head full of white hair.

"Oh yeah? She seems cool. Do you drink here often?" I say over the din of the bar. He gives us a disinterested look and with a limp wave of the hand says,

"I've been coming here since before you were born, back as far as the sixties."

"No way! I bet you've seen a few things in your time?" I ask curiously.

"I've seen some things. But that's all over now. Now it's just me and this glass of wine." He says, returning his gaze to the glass in front of him. He closes the door to the conversation now and huddles back over his wine. We don't exist anymore, we're just a memory like everything else in his life. The wine slowly drains itself and the buzz is strong now. Our new friend keeps stealing looks back at us and smiling. Thirty minutes pass by in seconds and soon she's heading our way.

"Hey, let's get out of here and get that drink." She says while pulling on a coat hanging near the door. We quickly get up to follow.

"Have a goodnight." I say to the mole skin man. He lifts an eye to me, grunts and nods then resumes his huddle.

"Wow, Paul never says hi to anyone. I saw you talk to him. What did he say?" She asks as we burst through the doors to the waiting street.

"He just said he had a lot of memories. Who is that guy? Looks interesting." I ask.

"That guy is Paul Kantner from Jefferson Airplane. He must like you, he usually just ignores everyone." She says while leading us up to the street back towards Washington Park and North Beach. Sara and I look at each other in shock and laugh.

"That's wild, you'd never think it to look at him. Although his eyes do seem kind of ancient and wise, maybe a little sad." I say reflectively as our new friend leads us out into the night. It's almost midnight and we pass by a few crowded bars before she turns to us and says, "I'm not really feeling a bar. Do you guys want to just grab a bottle at a shop somewhere? We can take it down to the pier and have some sneaky drinks."

"That sounds like a great idea, and our van is parked nearby." Sara says with a thick tongue. She's a tiny human and by now half her body weight is liquor and wine.

"Oh, you guys have a van? That's awesome. Ok I know a spot." She says, grabbing Sara's hand and pulling her down a street towards the bodega on the corner of Stockton and Columbus. We pass by a few drunks heading back towards the Vesuvio and one turns around to whistle at the girls. Our new friend flips them the bird and laughs while linking arms with Sara.

The door to the bodega swings open with a jingle and we enter into the store with high shelves crowded with a hundred different sundry items. On the back wall is a cluttered case full of liqueurs and various bottles of wine and spirits. The girls move in a straight line right to the bottles of liqueurs and Sara laughs after our friend whispers in her ear. She looks back at me and smiles.

"We should get this bottle of Chartreuse and maybe a little more Champagne. What do you guys think?" She asks, now standing with her hands on her hips in mock concentration. The bottle filled with green liquid sits dusty on the middle shelf, not touched in months or maybe years.

"Chartreuse, what's that? It looks deadly." I say laughing.

"It's what French prostitutes drank in 19th century Paris." She says matter of factly.

"Let's take two then." I say, half joking.

"Good idea, they are tough to find." She says and not hearing my sarcasm grabs two of the bottles filled with a mysterious green and heads to the cooler.

"Ok and let's grab that bottle of Champagne dear." She says while pointing to Sara to grab a bottle of Moet Chandon that's sitting on the top shelf of the refrigerator. Why not, I think, as Sara grabs the bottle and we head to the counter.

"Oh, should we grab snacks?" She asks, turning back to the shelves full of random bits.

"We have oysters and salmon and cheese and crackers back at the van." Sara offers shyly.

"Oysters! Yes, that sounds perfect." She says with a coy smile. Her energy is infectious. She has that cosmic presence where everything she touches turns to gold. I imagine her as a wood nymph, flitting through the forest turning dead things into vibrant, pulsating life. We practically skipped to the counter to purchase our wares and before we knew it we were back out onto the street laughing.

Time flies as we wander our way down Stockton, back towards the Embarcadero and Fort Mason. The way is well lit and by the time we get back to Fisherman's wharf the crowds have thinned to just a scattering of drunken travelers making their way back to whatever fancy hotel they came from. We walk up to the low concrete wall where the swimmers freeze and she jumps up and like a tight roper walks with one foot in front of the other. The bridge and the hills are full of sparkling lights that reflect onto the water in dancing images.

"Let's open that chartreuse and sit and look at the bay for a while." She says while balancing on one foot in some strange and quirky ballet movement. I look at Sara and her eyes are sparkling, following the every move of our new friend.

"Yeah I'm ready, I had forgotten how beautiful the bay is at night." I say as I uncork the Chartreuse and bring it to my lips. The green liquid has a viscous quality to it, almost thick with pungent aromas and a taste that hits you like a freight train. It tastes like Christmas morning if you were a Victorian lamplighter or an undertaker maybe. I could see someone substituting this for formaldehyde or liquid mercury. I cough after a long swig and immediately feel the warm rush of the booze.

"Isn't it amazing? It has this really delicious herbal goodness to it. Like you're drinking a witches brew." She says while taking the bottle, balancing on the opposite foot and taking a long swig.

"By the way, I'm Rosalyn." She says laughing and handing the bottle to Sara.

"I'm James and this is Sara." I say.

Sara takes a sip and grimaces but then smiles and hands the bottle back to me. She lets out a small cough and Rosalyn laughs joyfully.

"So tell me about this odyssey. Where are you guys headed?" She asks after sitting down, crossing her legs and leaning in to offer us her full concentration. The lights are glowing behind her and we also lean forward as if our journey is a secret.

"We're headed to Mexico and from there we have no idea. We got the van after working on a pot farm up north after our car broke down. It's all about taking a shot at the cosmic spark." I say while taking another, smaller sip of the glowing liqueur. Rosalyn's eyes glow a little and I pass her back the bottle.

"It's an old ambulance that we converted into a camper. Sort of looks like a giant marshmallow." Sara says laughing. A chill wind picks up and the girls huddle closer together. The stars are being replaced by heavy rain clouds and the last remaining wanderers are picking up their pace to head back to vehicles and shelter.

"Tut, tut looks like rain." Rosalyn says while standing up and balancing again, bowing towards the sea. Another strong gale sweeps through the concrete amphitheater and we all stand up to prepare for the rain.

"Let's go to your van for drinks and oysters." She says while taking Sara's arm and walking ahead. I trot up next to her and link my arm with hers while my other hand holds the bottles, clinking in the plastic bag. We start skipping up the hill towards Fort Mason like adventurers on the yellow brick road, quickly now, were under the giant eucalyptus trees and fast approaching the hostel. A few lights are still on and you can see people partying in their rooms. The girls are locked into a conversation about Sara's shawl and we avoid being distracted as we speed past. The first few drops of rain have started to fall and just as we leave the shade of the eucalyptus a holy deluge begins. The sky opens up and releases a billion metric tonnes of water. Our soaked clothes stick together as we separate and run towards our awaiting van. We can see her in the distance, parked right where we left her.

"Ahoy! I see the Marshmallow now." Rosalyn cries, pointing an excited finger at the van that's tucked away in the secret parking lot behind the Conservancy.

We run up to the van and I give Sara the bag of booze while I fumble with the keys. The water is pouring down and there's nothing to do but to pile into the van in a heap, soaking wet and laughing while trying to unstick from each other as I close the sliding door. Sara quickly grabs our lantern and the light sends a warm glow to reveal the details of our new home.

"Oh wow, this is really cool. I love the carpet. I am soaking wet, do guys mind If I take my shirt off. I know we just met and all." She says laughing and giving us her famous smile.

"Yeah I think that's a good idea. Let's all take off our shirts." I say drunkenly. Sara is laughing so hard she's practically in tears as Rosalyn quickly removes her shirt to reveal a perfect porcelain body with a black lacy bra and a belly button piercing. She turns and finds Sara struggling with hers so she helps her with the rest and gives her a quick peck on the lips. Laughing the whole time. Sara looks over at me with a smile so full of loose pleasure that I almost think that it's about to happen when,

"Oh I want oysters. Do you guys have tabasco and lemon?" She asks, distracted and looking over at me as I pull off my soaking wet hoodie and t-shirt.

"Yes! Good idea. They are just behind Sara in the cooler. I'll grab the shucker and the platter. We should have lemons and tabasco as well." I say while rummaging under the bed for the platter. I hear a loud POP and it's Sara popping the champagne.

"Do we need glasses for the champagne?" Sara asks with a giggle.

"No way, let's just neck it and eat oysters right out of the shell like hedonists and lovers." She says with a voice full of poetry.

I love how this girl thinks, I say to myself right after Sara passes me the bottle. Taking a swig of the bubbles and passing it to Rosalyn I find the oyster shucker and reach for the ice cold canvas bag filled to the brim with oysters. Setting the bag down on a plastic bag I reach in for the first of the enormous mollusks. It is the size of my hand and rough and salty and full of barnacles and strange things.

"Look at that sea monster!" She says in wonder at the massive oyster. Having shucked a few hundred oysters in my day I expertly jab the shucker into a crevice and begin to pry open the shell. A few moments of struggle and then the oyster pops open to reveal the perfect, erotic, clean flesh. I hand it to Rosalyn and she squeezes a lemon wedge that Sara cut and puts a few dabs of tabasco and expertly slurps it down in one sensual gulp. I immediately shuck another and hand it to Sara who repeats the process. Soon I have a few more shucked and ready to go. Rosalyn stands up in the van holding the Champagne, her tight wet jeans clinging to her legs and her slender waist gleaming in the light. Her wet hair is everywhere now and her lips part to bless the meal.

"I bless thee, oh oyster of the sea
For I will always love thee
With a splash of spice and a swig of wine
I bring it all down, even the brine."

We cheer and all take hearty draughts of the french bubbles. Sara builds a nice plate of lemon wedges, soft cheeses and dumps the whole box of crackers onto the plate, placing it onto a shelf that holds our small kitchen. I crawl up to the front to grab our small, portable radio and switch it on to a station playing tropical jazz and the party really kicks off. The girls are talking about the carpet again and I'm shucking more oysters. The music is picking up its pace and I can almost cut the tension in the room with a knife.

"Ok there's three oysters left. Let's all take them at the same time and then wash them down with the rest of this Champagne." I say, now so inebriated that I can barely contain myself. We all reach for our last oysters and after preparing them, look each other in the eyes and down them and all their delicious clean, salty goodness. The music slows down to a smokey tune about loving Porgy and the bottle is passed and emptied. Sara starts to shiver and Rosalyn huddles closer wrapping her drunken arms around her tiny waist.

"Let's get these wet clothes off you dear, you're so cold. Come, let's go under the blankets and get you warm." She says while standing Sara up and softly running her hands down her shivering body, undoing the button on her wet jeans and peeling them off to expose Sara's perfect mound hidden behind dark lace that matches Rosalyn's bra. She kisses her quickly on her stomach and stands up to smile. Sara drops down and does the same to Rosalyn to reveal nothing but smooth skin and the sweet, soft warmth. They both start laughing and push past me to jump in the bed, immediately hiding under the covers laughing and giggling and squirming like silky eels in a spellbound net.

"Hey, you. Mr Odyssey. Get in here." Rosalyn says while poking her head out from under the covers. I glance around, gathering in the clutter and fun of the evening. The rain is still pouring down and the wind howls and the radio plays something sweet as I pull off my trousers and get ready to jump into the fiery pits of sin. I pause for a moment, to really take it all in. This is it, this is the magic.

Chapter 11

The Morning After

The first light of morning trickled in through the half closed curtains of the van. The wind was still whistling through the small cracks and three disheveled heads emerged from under the covers. Traffic on Bay st is already starting and the noises of the city return. Sara, her head resting on Rosalyns naked chest, gives out a huge yawn and stretches long so that her toes poke out from the bottom of the bed. Our new friend is sandwiched in the middle, her eyes flutter open and that coy smile of hers shines new light into the dim cabin. I'm not quite awake yet, my head is already starting to feel heavy, like a block of raw iron ore. Through half open eyes I watch the girls sit up, looking around to survey the damage. Rosalyn still has that perfect smile and Sara looks shy and lovely in the half light as they pull on their shirts. I let out a groan and the girls turned to me to laugh.

"Wake up sleepy head, time for breakfast!" Rosalyn says, ripping the blankets off and jumping on top of me. She playfully bites my nipple and tugs at my hair.

"Ok, ok I'm up. What time is it anyways, let's go back to bed for the rest of the week." I say, groggy and ready for more. The adventures of the previous night seem unreal and far away like looking into a long tunnel and straining to see where it ends. The van has lost any semblance of being neat and tidy with an empty bottle of champagne and bits of crackers and loose wet clothes everywhere. Sara, still half asleep, grabs a trash bag and starts to quickly gather some of the trash strewn from the driver's seat to the very back of the van. Oyster shells and wrappers from the cheese and crackers fall into the bag while Rosalyn struggles with her still wet jeans.

"I have a dry pair you can have if you want," Sara says happily.

"Yes please, that would be nice."

"So, where should we have breakfast?"

"I know a place out in the mission, best breakfast burritos in the city. It's an instant cure for a hangover. Plus I live nearby so you guys can drop me off on your way out of town."

"Don't you just want to run away with us to Mexico?" Sara asks, half joking but not.

"Ha, I'd love to, but I need to work and I have a goldfish." She says, lighthearted and with joy.

"Maybe I'll come down in a couple weeks to visit you if I can get a fish sitter." She says while whistling and organizing her things. I let out a small laugh and she gives me a mock dirty look and her famous pouty lips. Sara is dressed now and takes a long drink from a bottle of water. She rummages around and finds our bag of weed and quickly rolls a joint for the drive. I reach for the water and finish it off in one long gulp. Rosalyn throws me my jeans and in one motion I pull on my jeans and reach for my shirt. Dressed and ready with an aching head I jump into the driver's seat and turn the engine on to get the car warmed up and the heater running. The girls are sitting in the bed still talking about coffee and breakfast loudly until I get the drift.

"Babes, can you please hoist up all the curtains and batten the hatches, we're about to embark on the next epic journey. To the Mission and beyond!" I say with grandiose gestures. The girls look at me with heads half cocked and shaking their heads at my corniness set the van up for departure.

"Does anyone want to sit up front with me or am I just a chauffeur now?" I ask laughing.

"Nope, you are our official chauffeur now, drive us to breakfast Mr Odyssey. And throw some music on." Rosalyn says laughing. I rummage about and find our Grateful Dead tape and shove it into the tape deck. The girls cheer as I back out into the road and start making my way back up Bay street towards the 101.

"Ok here we go, Sara light up that joint!" I shout over the sound of the engine and music. In a moment the lit joint is passed to me and the first puff brings relief to my raging head as we rumble down the road. Traffic is light at this early hour and we quickly find ourselves on the highway, passing the park and finally shooting out into the Mission District. The girls are sitting close and laughing while smoking the rest of the joint. On sharp turns they lean into each other for balance and play wrestle in the bed when the van speeds up to merge into traffic. Luckily the windows have a slight tint and our private world is still protected from prying eyes. The heady smell of cannabis, sex and spilled booze permeates and the music plays loud. I roll down the window to let in the fresh sea air and a clean feeling rolls over me like the clouds moving into the bay. Looking back at the girls in the rearview mirror I turn down the music and ask, "Ok so where do we go in the Mission? We're just about there."

"Taqueria El Farolito, it's just up ahead on the left. You can pull in behind these cars." She says, pointing to a bright yellow sign advertising all of the best foods. Tacos, burritos and quesadillas. And hopefully coffee. The weed dulled my headache but now I feel like I'm sitting in a cloud of booze, weed and three hours of sleep. I needed that inky black goodness and I needed it bad.

Pulling up to the curb outside the restaurant and the girls have already opened the sliding door before I can turn off the engine. With linked arms they stumble inside before I even exit the car and as I make my way inside I can hear them ordering.

"Three breakfast burritos with bacon por favor?"

"And three coffees."

"Wait, what did you guys get?"

"Trust me, you will like it."

How can you argue with a girl that beautiful and crazy. It's like arguing with the rain. You're only going to get wet so you might as well let it soak you. Taking our seats around a small circular table a waitress brings over our steaming coffees. The first scalding sip is the best, scorching my throat and reigniting the fires in my belly. In moments our food arrives, three giant burritos the size of small babies. The waitress struggles under the weight of them and lets out a sigh of relief as she passes them out to us. After surprised gasps from Sara and I, we slip into silence as we chow down like ravenous wild dogs after a long winter. Our booze addled organs finding relief in the thick bacon and scrambled eggs, wrapped with melted cheese, beans and crispy hash browns. I drown it in hot sauce and finish off my coffee, sitting back and patting my belly with both hands like a satisfied sea otter.

"That. Was. Amazing." I say slowly.

"Wow, I didn't even hear you say that about last night." Sara says laughing and chewing at the same time. Rosalyn nearly chokes and laughs so hard that the other customers are starting to stare. My cheeks glow coal hot and I laugh into my empty coffee cup. I start to feel a little sad that we'll be leaving our new friend behind and we meet eyes for a moment in between bites. A deep cosmic sensuality oozes from her and she reaches over and takes both of our hands in each of hers. We have a moment of silence, an onlooker might have thought we were praying. In a daze we make our way back outside near the van.

Rosalyn pulls us both in for a group hug.

"I loved last night, I hope we meet again. Now, go forth on your epic odyssey." She says grandly, giving us each a quick kiss and turning around on her heel to walk away. Her movements are cat-like, she confidently strides away and without looking back raises a hand to wave goodbye. In moments she disappears around a corner. Sara and I look at each other with half smiles and laugh.

"And just like that, she's gone." Sara says with a small hint of sadness.

"I wonder if we'll ever see her again?" I ask

"She gave me her contact info."

"When?"

"After you passed out, we stayed up talking in the front seat." She says, still looking down the street. A few raindrops start falling and we quickly clamber back in the van. Alone again in our new home, Sara starts to reorganize the clutter while I make the bed, tucking the sheets and blanket in tightly. In my life there are few greater pleasures than a freshly made bed. It doesn't take long to erase the signs of the night's adventures and before we know it we are buckled in and heading south on the 101. The windshield wipers driving away the spitting and sputtering drops of sky water. Soon we were passing San Francisco State University and the traffic picks up. The burrito did the job of subduing the hangover but now that we're back in traffic an anxious feeling creeps into both of our hearts as we struggle to find our way down the highway. Sara has our map splayed out onto the long dashboard and she's frantically looking for the turnoff for Highway 1.

"It should be any minute. I don't want to take the 280. It's too busy. Let's just take our time and go down the coast past Half Moon Bay." She says anxiously.

"Yeah, just tell me where we need to go. You're the navigator." I say, irritated at the moron ahead of me who keeps speeding up and slamming his brakes.

"Don't yell at me! I'm doing the best I can." She says, fighting back tears as the traffic picks up and a car honks at us to speed up. The 280 passes the airport and what was once a four lane highway turns into an eight lane highway. Cars screaming past to get to work or to the airport or to hell. Small vehicles skirting in and out of lanes doing their best to get just a few feet farther than the last guy. Like a great spring, stretching its metallic ringlets and rebounding as soon as it reaches its point of resistance. The same tiny car doing its best to pass me is now stuck in the opposite lane as we cruise by. We've left the aging beauty of the city behind us, and now it's just metal and concrete and angry commuters. But finally just ahead..

"There it is, make this turn. It's the 1!" Says the navigator, leaning forwards in her seat as to not miss out on the action. I immediately throw on my turn signal and in moments that feel like hours we exit the hectic stream of consciousness that is the 280 at nine o'clock in the morning. Instantaneously we are relieved of the madness. Like popping a zit or letting out an uncomfortable fart. Instant relief. We wind our way down towards the water and at reasonable speeds cruise towards Half Moon Bay and beyond.

"Good job. That was insane. Next stop is Half Moon Bay!" I say with renewed exuberance. The road has almost completely cleared of traffic and just a spattering of vehicles move with us down the coast. We pass through a small harbor town with fancy houses lining the hillside and wind our way around to begin the trek south on the coastal highway. Taking the 101 is much quicker but there's something romantic about the empty and much slower Highway 1. Winding our way past Pacifica and then on towards Davenport where we've always loved to stop and take in the quiet ocean views.

We've left behind the crowded roads and it's just us on this stretch of the highway. The hills on our left lead high into green pastures of redwood and meadow and on our left the raging, deep blue sea. So close to the cliffs and beach that we can almost taste the sea foam as it explodes onto the rocky shoreline. We're now driving through areas that start to look familiar to me. Only five years before I had spent two years living in Santa Cruz. It had been a very special period of my life where I was first exposed to the rhythm of the world. I was mostly just a dumb kid that only lived to surf and fall in love. One was not exclusive to the other. Growing up in southern California I had always loved the ocean. My first surfboard was a used, nameless six foot short board that was so battered that it could barely ride a wave. That never stopped me though, come rain or shine I was in the water. Sometimes very early and sometimes very late to avoid the crowds of much better surfers. For some reason it has never come easy to me. I had to paddle harder and try to find my timing more than the average surfer. But once you catch that first wave it's almost impossible to forget. One can almost relate it to sex or the first time you eat a really amazing meal. The ocean is a moving, breathing organism and to harness it for even a ten second wave ride is an unparalleled experience.

The whole of the ocean road now is coming back to me in waves of nostalgia. There, on the right is where I parked my jeep Cherokee, crawling in the back seat to fall asleep so that I could wake up early to find the perfect wave. Not too far past that beach was the little store that sold those cheap turkey sandwiches that had kept me alive for the weekend trip five years before. For a second I was tempted to pull in and see if they still made them but we were eager to make it to our next camping spot. The traffic of the city had drained us and there was no way we'd be going much further than Santa Cruz tonight. We were getting close to the city and the traffic picked up just a touch so that there were a few more vehicles on the road. Given that it was winter we were lucky to not have to deal with the hordes of tourists that summer brings from the city. These were just cars headed to work and given the relaxed vibes of the city didn't seem to be in much of a hurry. We love unhurried traffic. I'd prefer to slowly make my way down just about any road. I hate feeling rushed and love taking in the scenery. We had left behind the stretch of sand dunes and beach and now we're reentering into a lush forest of mixed redwood and coastal pine with the ocean hidden from view. Coming up on the turn for the University we laugh bitterly at a few students making their way up to their expensive cages.

Before we know it we're on that colorful street full of surf shops and restaurants that leads us into the downtown area of Santa Cruz. Pacific ave and the famous boardwalk are the usual destinations but not today. We navigated on familiar roads back to the highway and in just a few minutes were out of the city and continuing south.

"I'm thinking well go to the state park outside of Watsonville to spend the night. There's some great campsites and we can walk down to the beach for a bonfire if we want". I say while shifting lanes to avoid a massive truck merging onto the highway. Sara's eyes are focused on the road, the traffic has picked up and the 1 is once again full of commuters. She nods and then sighs. "I don't want to, but we need to get some supplies. Let's stop at a store somewhere." We're coming up on Capitola now, the town I had lived in while going to a local community college. I knew it well and turned off on 41st ave to make our way down towards the Whole Foods that would have everything we'd need.

Driving down this road brought back a flood of memories. Five years before I had struggled down the avenue a thousand times. I had moved there to follow my then girlfriend into college. I struggled to focus on studies and was more of a beach bum than anything else. I delivered pizzas and was so poor that I mostly lived out of my jeep. I don't know how I made it. There had been a million misguided adventures. A few heartbreaks and some big time mistakes but it was an experience I would never forget. Being back here brought a slew of emotions. Some sad and some very happy.

We quickly found the shopping complex that had Whole Foods and a few other stores. Pulling into the parking lot I felt the immediate dread of being thrust back into society. In our van and on the road we were quarantined and separate from the rest of the world. In our minds it was a land yacht and we were adrift on a dangerous ocean. When we made landfall, who would we find waiting for us in the shadows?

"I really don't want to go in there." I say, gazing forlornly at the crowded shopping center.

" I can just go in, grab some dinner quickly." She said, gathering her things she leans over and kisses my cheek. The door opens and shuts and she's strutting confidently into the market.

The anxiety I feel when shopping in crowded spaces can be described as a combination of claustrophobia and a mental heart attack, then add a few sprinkles of existential terror and a dash of nausea. Shopping centers are horrible places. I'd imagine in the past the experience was a little more rewarding but today's generation is only about getting in and out as soon as possible. It can be downright cutthroat at times. Old ladies are the worst, they've had enough of your shit and they just want the steak you've been staring at indecisively for the last five minutes. Move out of my way sonny boy, I ain't got that much time left. You push your cart skillfully to avoid all of the mouth breathers and mongoloids but you barely make it out with your life. So, needless to say, I was happy Sara was doing the shopping.

Watching the flow of traffic brought back so many memories. Every other car seems to have a surf rack or bike rack on top of the car. All kinds of tanned characters walking towards the ocean for a surf. Capitola is a colorful old town that has a history with alternative people. Sunny and bright homes are just moments from some of the best surfing in the United States. It's had a varied past. Once a failed whaling port, now it's mostly just students, hippies and inherited wealth.

Looking back at the store I can see Sara hurrying past an older couple blocking the door with a mobility scooter. She's smiling ear to ear and shaking her head. Jumping out to open the door she laughs and says,

"Well, you would have hated that experience."

"Ha, why? What happened?

"Just assholes. I got some good stuff though. They had really nice local halibut." She says while jumping into the car and opening the cooler to dump fresh ice and add our dinner. In the bag she had a bag of salad and some fresh brie along with a pound of fresh halibut wrapped in butcher's block paper. A fresh loaf of sourdough bread and some hummus and a lemon. It would be a small feast and the first time we would use the new camp stove equipment that Aldon had given us.

"Oh cool, you got those special shiitake mushrooms." I say as I continue to rummage through the bag of goodies.

"Yep, they were expensive but I wanted us to have something good tonight." She says while looking through our tapes to find some music for the road. Grabbing one and popping it into the tape deck while I climb into the driving seat to start up the van. I turned the engine over and we're back on the Cabrillo Highway. Leaving behind my treasured memories and glad to have escaped the crowds. The highway has thinned out now and there's not quite as much traffic as before. Were leaving behind the whitewashed surfer villages for the other side of the tracks. Watsonville and all its hispanic treasures. People overlook it because from the surface it appears to be a hectic industrial city famous for street crime and rival Mexican gangs. For years it was passed over by tourists headed to either Santa Cruz or Monterey Bay. Thus allowing it to create generational cultural treasures. Some of the finest Mexican food in the state can be found here, tucked away into industrial areas where laborers can easily find them. Inland you have factories and a pretty downtown area, decorated in the colonial Spanish style and as you get closer to the sea you are surrounded by an ocean of strawberry fields. They stretch as far as the eye can see from the border of the city to the sea. Undulating hills of tidy green rows dotted with millions of blood red strawberries. If you've eaten a strawberry in the US it's likely it came from Watsonville. The town has magic underneath its gritty exterior. So many colors waiting to burst forth when the time is right.

"Ok, there's San Andreas drive. Well turn here to make it to Sunset Beach Campground." She says pointing to the sign. We quickly turned off and headed down the road towards Manresa State Beach where I would go to escape all of the crowds. The waves were never very good here. Often too fast and blown out but on occasion a good set would come through and you'd have it all to yourself. In the old days I would just sneak into the parking lot early in the morning before the park ranger would arrive. I'd paddle out just as the sun was lighting up the world and stay until the first surfers arrived later in the morning. It was early afternoon and the skyline was gunship gray as we passed Manresa. The lot looked different this time. It looked older and tired. Only a few cars parked and the ranger station seemingly abandoned. We were eager to get to our campsite so we continued on, making the sharp turn and finding ourselves smack dab in the strawberry fields. All around us and in front as we slowed down to take in the scenery. Sara had found a tape with old Spanish flamenco music and we turned it up to add to the experience. The sky was gray but the temperature wasn't terrible so we rolled down our windows to let in the fresh smell of the sea and the loamy earth.

The van rumbles past the acres and acres of sloping strawberry fields and soon comes upon the sign and turnoff for the state park. Another long, ambling road headed back towards the sea now and the cliffs that hang above it. Pulling up we noticed that the park ranger station where you normally fill out your campsite info to pay the fee was empty. On approach the sign read that it closed at four thirty. It was now four forty five. Putting the car into park but leaving the engine running I jumped out to check the instructions. The sign explained that it was self service and that someone would be around after nine a.m to check that we had paid. Great, I thought. Should be out of here before nine then. Chuckling to myself and grabbing a form to fill out and to place in my window.

"The office is closed. We have to pay and put our form in that box by nine a.m tomorrow." I say while buckling back in and throwing the car into gear.

"Ha, well, we should be out of here by nine." She says laughing at our good fortune. Laughing with our bellies we pull away from the ranger shack and wind our way up the cliff and through the forest to the first set of campgrounds that hug the cliffside. Cozy, open spots large enough for just about any vehicle and shaded by Monterey pine and Pacific madrone trees. There is almost no one in the entire campground and nearly every site is free.

"That spot looks cozy, right there under the trees with the path to the beach." She says pointing. Not seeing a better place I quietly pull in and turn off the engine, leaving the music to play while I unwind from the adventure of the last few hours after leaving San Francisco. I get that weird warp drive feeling as if the road is still moving underneath us and the world outside expands and then contracts while the engine ticks and tocks. I unbuckle and give a good stretch.

"Well, we made it. There's even a hot shower a few campsites down. I might go for it before I get too lazy." I say after jumping in the back to grab my towel and toiletries bag.

"Yeah that's perfect. I'll get everything set up for dinner. Hurry up though because I want a shower too." She says. You can see her humming a quiet tune and primping and plumping the cushions. Now, I could be wrong of course and instead of a quiet, nameless tune it's a song about servitude and in her head she's imagining my head on a spike next to all of the other lazy husbands of the world. The husband is widely considered to be the laziest of all earthling creatures. Coming in second is the sloth and tabby cats.

Getting out of the van and surveying our territory I noticed just one SUV on the other side of the campsite. They shouldn't be too much bother I think as I trot the couple hundred feet to the public bathroom and shower. It's one of those typical concrete bunker showers that are in every single state park in the country. Four separate showers in between the bathrooms and all of them are available. I choose the closest one to me and close the door behind me. It's a tiny room, just big enough to undress and hang my clothes before standing on the cold concrete. The hot water works and I'm washing off the grime of the day and of the leftover adventures from the previous evening. It was hard to believe that all of that had happened less than 24 hours ago. I couldn't help but think about Rosalyn and how absolutely mad that entire experience was. And how delicious and perfect at the same time. I wondered if we would ever see her again. I let the water run over me until it goes cold because there's nothing better than a hot shower at the end of a stressful drive. You need to wash the sweat of fear and anger off you so that you can fully unwind. Drying off and redressing I plunge back into the mild afternoon light. The clouds have worn off a bit and long strips of lenticular clouds and deep, frozen blue sky shroud overhead. It will be dark in a few hours and the light is already changing. The walk back is short and I can hear music coming out of the giant marshmallow van. In the distance where the SUV was parked is an empty lot. Maybe we drove them away, I think to myself.

The van is parked under a low hanging madrone tree and Sara has hung a string of faery lights on the easy to reach branches. Our van is parallel to the road and we have our own, snug, private space with a picnic table and an in-ground grill. Sara has pulled out our two folding chairs and the two burner grill is hooked up to a can of propane and safely situated on the picnic table. Our side door is open and the fairy lights are connected above the open door to bring a comfortable circle of overhead light. She's sitting with her legs dangling and a smile on her face. In her delicate hand she holds one of the crystal sherry glasses that Aldon had given us from the bowels of his garage. In the glass is a cube of ice and the bright green liquid of the Chartreuse from the night before.

"Oh wow, this place looks great. I forgot about the Chartreuse." I say happily.

"Yeah we have like two bottles of the stuff, plus the unopened bottle of Champagne." She says excitedly holding the ornate bottle of green French whore juice. She has completely unwound, a smile that I think of sometimes on my darkest days stretches across her face. She lets out a squeak as I rush forward to embrace her. Picking her up and twirling her around while she holds the Chartreuse in one hand like a rodeo star.

"This is such a cozy spot. I could live here forever under the trees." She says dreamily. I put her down and spin her one handed. We laugh and sit together on the plush carpet of our new home, our legs dangling and dancing.

"Ok let's open that Champagne then." I say laughing.

"No, can we save it for dinner please. It will go perfectly with the fish and mushrooms. I have a plan." She says seductively.

"Here, have some Chartreuse, it's actually pretty great. It feels exciting to drink it, thinking of Rosalyn." She says in a hushed tone. She reaches under the bed and produces a matching glass and the bottle of chartreuse. Holding it like a pirate she pours me a healthy shot and hands it to me with sin in her eyes. We sat for a while listening to our Spanish music and drinking our fancy french whore juice. The Chartreuse feels exactly like it looks. It's thick and completely alien on your tongue. You will have never tasted anything like it. Distilled by the monks of the Chartreuse monastery in eastern France it is a strange and mysterious liquid. It sure goes down easy I think. Sara is putting a table cloth down and soon a full spread appears. Fresh sourdough bread and brie cheese with a can of sardines and a few little olives in their briny goodness. The brie spreads easily and a little tapenade of sardines and olive make for the perfect hor d'oeuvre. Washing it down with the herbal headiness of the chartreuse and we are in heaven.

Sara is in her element now. She's in her Bossa Nova groove and there's sure to be sorcery and magic. Unwrapping the butcher block paper reveals two thick, pale filets of halibut. She places the fish on a plate and brings out the cutting board to chop the onions, garlic and mushrooms.

"Light the stove please and put the cast iron skillet on the grill." She commands. She's not being mean, she just knows what she wants and her command carries the weight of an Army General. I snap to and bring the skillet to the camp stove and settle it onto the grill. With a wave of her hand she drops a chunk of the good butter that Sharon had given us on our last day and a sprinkle of fresh herbs that appear from nowhere. The butter quickly melts with the herbs and she drops the Halibut, skin down onto the cast iron. Her dark, curly hair drapes around her face that is tight with concentration. She drops the onions, garlic and mushrooms on one side of the skillet and soon the most delicious smells are permeating from our cozy campsite.

"That smells amazing and this Chartreuse is strong. No wonder that happened to us last night. I can't believe we were just in China Town. God, we went to Sam Woes didn't we?" She asks in wonder.

"Do you want to talk about what happened?" I whisper.

"No, it was perfect. I have no complaints. Do you?" She says with her head down, watching the food cook.

"No, it was all so wonderful."

The late afternoon quickly turned into early evening and the fairy lights are sparkling now against the darkening sky. In the distance the waves are crashing against the long stretch of sandy beach and our radio plays soft melodies deep into the night…

Chapter 12

El Camino Real

When the small group of Spanish explorers first descended on Monterey Bay they were full of scurvy and mutinies thoughts. For months they had been led north by great men, men of faith and vision, no matter what the cost. Father Junipero Serra, the expedition's spiritual leader, was convinced that Monterey would be their new capital. Previous adventurers had praised the Bay as the most beautiful in all the world and Serra was eager to see it be blessed with his dream to build a church and to convert the local Neophytes. But the famous Bay was nowhere to be found. Upon first gazing at the beautiful sloping beach the weary soldiers mistook it for something else. Thus leaving it behind and reporting back to a disappointed friar and allowing the Bay to remain unchanged for just a moment longer.

Waking up to the quiet of the park was a pleasure after the last several days of traffic and driving. I wanted to imagine that it was in this very spot that Captain Figueras of the Portola expedition had slept.

Parked in our cozy little den of good food and the warmth of each other.

Was it love at first sight? To gaze out upon an empty stretch of sand and tall bluffs covered in velvety green vegetation. I'd like to think a tear was shed and the sign of the cross made as they counted their blessings to have witnessed such simple beauty. Maybe it reminded them of their distant homes in Spain. Where nervous family members waited to hear of their unlikely survival. We had found a book detailing father Junipero Serra and the Portola expedition of 1769 at a roadside tourist attraction coming down the 101. We were hooked and it was now going to be a heavy focus on our way down the El Camino Real. There were twenty one missions that the Spanish explorers had built to both govern and convert the region known as La California. The most recent addition to the kingdom of Spain. Each mission was designed for both holy congregation and military advantage.

Here on these great bluffs the explorers had camped, hoping desperately to find a Bay that was quite literally in front of them. They were lost. Were we? Had we made the right decision to continue south and to Mexico? Should we just find a town to live in and find jobs and pay bills and join the ranks of the modern man? We had just enough money to get into an apartment and find a normal routine. My head was spinning with questions when I woke early to the sound of the crashing waves. Sara was still sleeping soundly as the sun was just beginning to light up the mountains in the east. I carefully got out of bed and pulled a shirt on and some shorts. Opening the sliding door quietly and stepping out into the cool, wet morning. We had left very little clutter from the night before. It was easy to just fold up our stove and tuck it away under the bed. The fairy lights were still hanging from the trees. Reaching back into the van to grab a hoodie and slipping on my sandals. It was time for an early morning walk. Clear my head and help find some direction and context. The van was still quiet except for the soft breathing of the woman.

Walking past the entrance to the campground and to the edge of the bluff brings you to a steep and rickety wooden staircase that leads down to the beach. Easy going down but a pain to come back up. I needed the exercise, driving all day atrophies your muscles. From my vantage point, making my way down the stairs you could see almost all of Monterey bay. From Santa Cruz to the Moss Landing power plant. The beach stretches in a smooth half circle from point to point. Trotting down the damp stairs and gazing out onto the foggy early morning tide I noticed one or two other humans. Each person seemingly lost in their own world.

The cool sand of the beach awkwardly meets my sandals and I take them off to hold while I struggle through the thick sand to the harder more compact sand where the water shows its mark. It's completely quiet, a soft stillness permeates over the slow moving tide. Each small wave sends a fan of slow moving crystal clear water over the dark sand. The waves reach out to touch my feet and to envelop them for a moment before the ocean pulls its icy tendrils back to the sea. It's winter and the water here was never warm. It sends a chill up my spine that both refreshes me and makes me long for the warmth of the van. Here and there a few seabirds dart in and out of the water, looking for food and adventure. A small group of sanderlings, move in perfect unison up and down the surf, needling their pointy noses into the sand to slurp out crustaceans and weird slimy things.

It's fun to feel the slippery sand under my feet and to feel the ocean's gentle pull. Pausing for a moment here and there to gaze back up onto the bluffs I can almost imagine those early explorers, starving and cold and far away from the warm waters of their homeland. For as many reasons that you can hate the early colonists there're just as many reasons to admire their tenacity and courage. Their many ignorances would lead to the decimation of the native population. A population that for the most part welcomed them into their villages with open arms. It's easy to think of the natives being savage and dumb. But then they also brought a system of roads and organized trade. If the world had never been colonized where would it be today? Would it really be a better place? History happened and the only thing we can do is honor the memories and try and do better next time. The natives that called this area home were simple people. Their focus was on survival and tribal success. They had no literature or collected music. Maybe a chant here and there but in Europe where the invaders had come from, Mozart was already starting to conduct symphonies. The Spaniards portrayed them as neophytes and mongrels. Unclothed and uneducated. A nomadic godless people that would benefit greatly from the Governance of Spain and the holy baptisms of the Catholic church. The tribes that saturated the coastline were an organized people that lived in peace and harmony with most of their neighbors. Northern and Central California had such an abundance of wildlife and rich, fertile soil for crops that there was almost no need for conflict or suspicion amongst those early people. And they had lived there for thousands of years. They were the Aptos and the Chumash and the mighty Tongva. Thousands of years of tradition would be wiped out as a result of those explorers. I often wonder if Europeans had just stayed within the boundaries of their own land, what would the world look like today? Would Africa be a thriving and united mega continent, sending engineers to the moon? Would the Cheyenne of the great plains be inventing life saving medicines from their teepees? Every action has an equal and opposite reaction. What you do now will cause a chain reaction of events that will ripple down through the ages. Our decision to go to Mexico and continue on our odyssey would have consequences.

The sun was quickly rising and the sky was turning into a spectacular scene of reds and purples and rays of light pouring through the chunky clouds. The tide was starting to move faster now and a small wind began to pick up offshore sending sea-foam flying. I had been walking for maybe twenty minutes and finally I passed the first of the two beachcombers. It was an elderly woman walking her small dog. She was gazing out onto the sunrise and we passed by each other without a word. It wasn't the type of environment to greet someone. This early in the morning we were here to contemplate not to communicate. I pulled the hood over my head and focused back on the waves. The sea was starting to get angry again. The sun had brought the wind and the peaked waves were getting to be explosive and blown out. It would be a struggle to surf here I thought. Short, quick bursts of wave energy with no curl or stride.

For a moment as the sun shone through the clouds I felt a shiver of excitement. It was silly to question the mission. We absolutely should go on this adventure. We don't have a mortgage, or kids or some bloated career to pursue. We have this moment and the next to do with what we will. I could feel the magic coursing through me as the cold water splashed around my ankles. With this new feeling of energy I turned around and half trotted half walked back up to the staircase and began the arduous and steep climb up the rickety steps. It didn't take long and it wasn't that bad. I have a lazy brain that forgets that a little exercise is good for you. The burning sensation in my thighs and the blood pounding in my temples was a good thing, I told myself as I sweated up the steps.

Reaching the top and bounding over the small hill that separated me from our campsite and almost running to wake up the beautiful girl in her warm nest of hair and blankets. I wanted to roar outside the van like a lion. My confidence would wipe away any remaining doubt. The van appeared and with it so did Sara. She was already up and taking down the fairy lights from the night before. A huge grin on her face and her eyes the color of fire.

"Hey, let's get moving. I can't wait to get on the road." She says. I trot up to her and pick her up in my arms and twirl her around. Setting her down gently and kissing her sweet, chilly face.

"I was just thinking about that myself. So you're happy with our adventure? You want to keep going?" I ask through my smile.

"Of course. I don't see how we can turn back now. There's too much to see."

"I was just worried that we were making the wrong decision and that maybe we should take some of the money we made and settle down." I say sheepishly.

Her face dropped into a deep frown and for a moment I thought I had ruined the moment. But then her eyes began to glow again and through the frown says,

"That's a terrible idea. I want to go south. Let's have an adventure."

"Yeah I think you're right. I just question our decisions sometimes."

"Well, just stop thinking about it and let's go. I want to get out of here before the ranger comes around to collect the fee." She says while packing away the lights. I fold up the chairs and do a quick sweep of the campsite. Always leave the site cleaner than how you found it was my dads motto. The wind picks up and we climb back inside the van. A quick look around to make sure everything is secure and the vans big engine rumbles to life after a quick turn of the key.

"Ok, so should we go down the coast towards Big Sur? Or back on El Camino Real and maybe stop at a vineyard and a mission?" I ask as I'm pulling out of our campsite.

She ponders the question for a minute as we quietly drive past the empty ranger station. Our decision to skip out on the fee wasn't out of malice but out of pure wildness. It made the voyage seem more exciting. Sometimes you just need to break a few rules in life.

"WOoooo! We made it." We shout in unison as our van hits the highway. In moments were accelerating up the coast, past the strawberry fields and artichokes that stretch in every direction for miles.

"I kind of want to go down the 101 towards the San Juan Bautista mission after reading about it last night. But Big Sur would also be pretty amazing." She says, still unsure of our direction.

"I like the sound of that. We can stop at the mission and then have lunch in Paso Robles before hitting up the vineyards. We can do Big Sur another time." I say with a confident smile. The book that we had found had detailed all of the missions from North to South.

Mission San Juan Bautista was only an hour's drive south according to our map. It would be a straight drive on the 101 or in days of yore called the El Camino Real, or, the Kings Highway. The missionaries and soldiers had established it to connect all of the Missions. Each mission was just a day's journey by horse. Thus ensuring an excellent network of fast trade and communication. The road is hot and dusty in the summer and cold and wet in the winter. On either side of the long road are the mighty Gabilan range and the Santa Lucia range of the Sierra Nevada. Mountains that in the spring are the most vibrant green and in the summer the color of the lion's that stalk its peaks. The hills turn golden and the farms and vineyards that stretch the length of the valley stand out in contrast. The valley runs from Salinas to Paso Robles and the Camino Real runs right down the middle of it. It has been a maintained road for almost two hundred and fifty years and it is saturated with many historical landmarks. From where we camped at Sunset State Park it's an easy drive inland to Salinas and from there we will be back on the 101 headed south. There are many hidden gems scattered throughout California, but only a few stand out like this magical region. Along with the Navarro Valley this is one of the other more underrated wine regions. For generations most of this land went unwanted. A few dusty outpost orchards and a handful of ancient vineyards and farms dotted the sparse valley.

The conditions are perfect here. You have the cold, wet winds from the Pacific Ocean and the hot and dry of the valley and Sierra Nevada's. Early European settlers from Italy and Portugal understood its value right away. The weather is the same in their home countries and the soil conditions are identical. Wine is not a new thing in this valley. The ancient and sacred grapes had been grown here by various waves of immigrants. From the Spanish missionaries to the Italians who came over in the late nineteenth century. It was remote and as the wine boom of the nineteen seventies roared into life the region lay shadowed by its northern cousins for decades. Then in the later part of the twentieth century the magic emerged. All of a sudden massive tracts of unused land started being bought up by smart, young vintners. People put in the work and now, fifty years later, it's a hot spot for adventure seekers and wine enthusiasts.

The Salinas Valley is nearly a hundred miles long. It begins in Salinas and ends in the Paso Robles area. One can easily imagine the early European explorers gazing out at the natural splendor of a region that would have easily resembled their homelands.

Our great big marshmallow home is cruising down the 101 after just a few minutes drive from the campground. It's taking us inland now, away from the winding coastal highway that heads past Big Sur. Its farmland as far as the eye can see on either side of the mountains. It's still early so the only traffic is the farmers headed to their crops.

"I love this sort of scenery." She says. Her eyes are locked on the Gabilan mountain range and the patches of farmland that criss-cross its landscape.

"It feels really empty, like ancient Mesopotamia. I wonder what kingdoms have come and gone here?" I ask, trying to focus on the road but distracted by the gentle beauty of the velvety green mountains.

"I don't know about all that. I just think it would be nice to have a little piece of land out here. Hide away from the world for a while." She says while fumbling around the cabin to find a new tape to put on.

"Maybe even grow some grapes and an orchard."

"And definitely some chickens and a goat, for the cheese."

"Ooo and maybe we'd have a big pond that I'd stock with trout."

"Sure, you can have your pond. I just want a few olive trees." She says laughing. Her Italian features are what you first notice about Sara. She has those dark eyes and thick curly hair. I joke that she's fifty percent olive oil and fifty percent parmesan. Less than a hundred years ago her family sailed from southern Italy to Ellis Isle to follow the American dream. Settling in Schenectady New York, her family had rarely traveled again. It was as if the wanderlust had died for a little while. They had found their little piece of the pie and it was good to sit still for a while. Sara was the first to cross the Pacific Ocean. The first to venture out into the darkness of the world. She was quiet but she was also mighty.

"God, can you imagine these early monks and explorers. I can just see them walking along this valley." She whispers.

"Right? I can see them in their brown habits and the little bald patch on their heads. What do they call that again?" I ask.

"A tonsure." She says confidently.

"What? No, it's something else. I think it's called a pate." I say laughing.

"Pate? That's something you spread on crackers you ninny. It's a tonsure. Trust me, I went to Catholic school." She says, chuckling to herself. She lifts her chin proudly and folds her arms over her breasts. Her smile is so pure and real that it would inspire whole armies to do their bidding. She reaches for the booklet on the Spanish missions and leaves through its pages.

"Ok so this first mission coming up is the Mission San Juan Bautista. I guess it's named after one of the priests who lived here." She says while flipping through the pages.

"Oh cool! It was also where they filmed parts of Vertigo. The Alfred Hitchcock movie I showed you last year." She says excitedly. "It's when they run in the bell tower. I guess the main feature of this mission is its three bells in a tower."

"Like Taco Bell?"

"Yes, like Taco Bell."

The road itself is in desperate need of repair. Cracks and crumbling edges. Every half mile or so a rusty old lamp post marks the El Camino Real. " You know, I think this is where Steinbeck based *The Pastures of Heaven.*

"I'd love to explore this area more someday." I say nostalgically.

"Ok we're coming up to San Juan Bautista, turn off here." She says pointing to the upcoming offramp. We exit and cruise down a road in need of repair following the old mission signs that point the way. The massive van bounces and squeaks down the lane and soon you can just see the red tiled roofs of the mission, poking out from a high adobe wall. We quickly park behind a group of other vehicles. The stone wall runs the length of a football field with several openings to allow entry to the mission. There are hanging flowers and plants ensconced in the wall and it has the feel of being in Spain.

"Ok, we're here! Let's go to the visitor center and then walk the grounds." I say.

I'm excited to be here. I love early colonial California history. My ancestors had crossed the great plains in a covered wagon to come to California during the gold rush and I loved to imagine a great grandfather stopping in this space, generations before. We rummage in the back for a moment so that Sara can put on a pair of jeans because it's gotten colder and I pull on a nicer sweater instead of my old Santa Cruz hoodie. Exiting the van through the sliding door and then locking it behind us we look for the entrance. Not far ahead a gap in the wall allows us to walk across the grounds facing the Mission in all its glory. Its elegant archways and rustic red tiled roof shout ancient words that you understand but can't explain. You know you are in a special place the moment you pass through the gap. Although not as old as some of the European or South American cloisters it still has an ancient feel to it. Like you're stepping back in time and can almost taste the cooking smoke and hear the clanging of the blacksmith.

The grounds are made up of church, mission and also a sprawling garden space. Walking through the garden and stopping to admire a few scattered statues and fountains we make our way to the door marked "gift shop". It's just after ten a.m and there isn't a single visitor in the store. Not that these missions were ever a tourist hot spot, on occasion you do get the odd tour bus or school group. But today there is no one. The store sits empty, sparsely decorated and just a few pamphlets and church paraphernalia. A rosary for sale and a dozen different saints embossed on colorful cards that say they cost a dollar.

"Hello, anyone here?" I ask loudly. There is an open back door and a tired and ancient lady emerges. She is stooped with age, her wrinkles so deep they almost form geological features on the surface of her face. She looks at us through horn rimmed glasses and shrugs her shoulders quietly.

"Hi, we wanted to take a tour of the mission and the grounds." I say awkwardly.

There is a pause and she looks at both of us, scrutinizing our appearance and with a huff, "It's three dollars a person. Please don't touch any of the artifacts in the museum." She says in a monotone voice. Handing us each a tattered pamphlet which includes a map marked with specific areas of interest. I reach into my pocket and fish out the cash handing her the approximate amount in one dollar bills. She makes a show of counting out the currency and without a word she points to the entrance to the mission.

"Hey thanks, have a great day. God Bless." I say with half a smile. She just grunts and turns back to hide in her little cave. The entrance to the mission is a narrow doorway with ancient wooden beams and plastered adobe. The first step through the door and our feet meet the cold, ancient foot-stones that weary neophytes once laid. The chamber runs the length of the building and you can see many rooms along the hall. Following the map on the pamphlet and with our feet sending echoes down the corridor we find ourselves in the rectory. Gazing up at the ancient Jesus and cross. Imagining the monks and natives worshiping together is a strange image. They were so different from one another. Thinking of the natives shuffling piously through the corridor made me a little sad. Imagine being forced to leave your world behind for an ordered, cold and confined space.

We were still alone as our footsteps echoed down the hard corridor. Making our way to the end where the centuries old chapel lay in quiet stillness. It was a long and simple room with pews lined neatly towards the front where the ragged Jesus hung from the cross. Looking down on us from his lofty position I wondered if he was judging us now. Did he know our sins?

"It's so cold in here." I say with a shudder.

"I know, it feels lonely. Like an empty place." She said, looking up at the ancient god.

"Do you think there was ever much happiness here?" I ask, gazing up at him and wondering.

"Maybe, like at weddings or the funerals of bad men." She says quietly.

I take her hand gently and lead her away from this holy space. It's not for us, not right now. We're still on that glorious path of sin and we are not ready to ask for forgiveness. Maybe the day will come, I think. There's a door that leads to a small museum full of artifacts. An ancient habit. A bible with its leather covering worn and faded and its pages so brittle and yellowed with time that even touching it might destroy it. And then the next room is a large and sparse room with the Holy Mothers image painted on a large canvas and hung between two small pillars that look like they belong in ancient Rome. Maybe they were once there. Maybe the monks carted those heavy stone structures all the way from Mexico, the dumb bastards. You have to give it to them, the Spaniards, they were tenacious creatures that believed so devoutly that they were willing to sacrifice their souls. Imagine these young conquistadors at St Peters gate, waiting to be judged. They've just died of scurvy, or starvation or an arrow to the fucking neck. They wave up at the saint, ready for judgment, knowing in their hearts that because they tortured a young native woman to death, to accept the ragged Jesus, that they'll be ushered straight onto the golden streets. St Peter just looks at them, shakes his head and pulls the lever and the young, starving, scurvy infested murderers drop screaming into the fiery pits of hell.

The room empties out onto the interior gardens. Green, even in winter. A few tall palm trees wave gracefully, poking their heads out over the tiled roof tops. The pamphlet says that this is where they grew crops and herbs and various flowers that made the monks happy. It's a peaceful space. Feels much better than in the stone cold buildings. I imagine the tortured neophytes, allowed for a few hours to stop their prayers and to come out and enjoy the sun and the smell of growing vegetation.

A few bright clusters of winter flowers glow against the short cropped grass. Clumps of cacti and other interesting specimens rest in raised beds. It's a long time ago now that the magic fingers of the mighty neophytes graced a trowel or gardening tool. I wonder who tends the garden now? Is it a monk or a state parks employee? Either way they both have medical and dental and probably a 401k. Lucky, I think.

The garden leads to where the famous tower of bells looks out towards an expanse of fields and then the mountains beyond. It's the most comforting part of the mission. It has a timelessness about it that seems innocent and reliable. Imagining the bells ringing out into the hills where the workers and soldiers were waiting for the reassuring sound. The sound that meant, time for worship, danger is coming and dinner is ready.

"It's a cool place, but it's also a little scary." She says as we walk back towards our home on wheels.

It has an effect on you, this ancient place of penance. You're left with all of the tough cosmic questions. A little joy, a little sorrow, a little fear. An empty space in the stomach that lingers long after a satisfying meal. We were eager to get back to our private world where we could hide from those questions for a little longer.

Walking across the broad lawn towards the wall where our home is safe and sound and suddenly a few drops of rain speckle our faces and shoulders.

"Tut tut, looks like rain." I say trying my best to mimic the way Rosalyn had sounded, looking up at the dark, angry clouds that have rolled in over the mountain range. Then, without any in between a billion gallons of water empties out onto us. We run and laugh our way across the lawn and into our vehicle. Quickly turning the key and driving away from the dead place where ancient history is locked away behind glass and hung up on walls for everyone to see after paying their three dollars.

*   *   *

The Camino Real empties into the Paso Robles city limits almost suddenly, with no warning. From an outward appearance it is a nothing place. A handful of restaurants and a few industrial buildings would be all that you'd see if you were just passing through. Peak under the surface and we were surprised at what we found. New wineries and tasting rooms seem to open up every month and the downtown area has definitely grown from the last time that I was here, when it was just a dusty old agriculture hub.

"We should find a good vineyard now. Grab some wine before heading back to the coast." I say, looking around for a sign to follow.

"I've read that there's a tasting room that's built like a castle with a moat and everything." She says, flipping through a vineyard pamphlet we had picked up at the gas station near the Mission.

"Ok so we have to turn on the 46 West and head back towards the coast and we should see it off the highway."

"Sounds good to me. I'm ready to wet the old whistle." I say, licking my lips and making a face.

"Why are you so weird?" She says, shaking her head.

"I was born this way, can't be helped." I say, reaching over to pinch her leg. She smacks my hand away and we laugh for a moment as we drive through the faceless city.

Paso Robles is a small town and before we know it the green highway sign for the 46 West is approaching. Making an easy turn we carry on down and back towards the coast. The nasty weather we experienced at the Mission seems to have abated or moved further north because the sun is now pouring through the big puffy clouds that are coming in off the coast. It's very rural here. The brownish gold scrub grass of winter is just starting to have patches of green break through. On either side of the highway are large hills covered in oak trees and scrub brush. At first glance it's an unassuming region although I imagine that spring here would be lovely. Pulling past a slow moving semi truck we almost miss the turn for Tooth and Nail and make a hard right that dislodges some of our gear. Up on the hill, away from the road is a large, turreted white castle that looks like something out of a cheesy movie about unicorns and knights of the round table. A large moat with bright green water surrounds the castle and in front of the moat is a sprawling parking lot that has just a few cars parked in it.

There is a path that leads you over the moat and up a small flight of stone steps and you're in the outer courtyard of the castle. We had quickly left the van, eager for a tipple and some advice on where we should go next. It was off season and the few cars in the parking lot must have just been Tooth and Nail employees because no one was sitting in the courtyard. The yard was beautifully decorated in the style of a Tuscan villa. Colorful plants and dangling flowers are strewn from a wooden gazebo and just as we approached the door a middle aged woman greets us with a smile.

"Hi there, table for two?" She asks with a charming smile.

"Yes please, we were hoping to do a tasting." I say

"No problem, the tasting is ten dollars each and we also do small plates of food." She says while grabbing two menus and leading us to a cozy table near a heat lamp. The warmth of the lamp is inviting even though it's only sixty degrees out and the sun is still shining. After sitting us she informs us that our server will be with us shortly and we are left with the menus and the unique setting.

"This place is wild."

"Yeah it's probably the most unique vineyard so far. It looks pretty fake but it's still cool." She says

"Let's grab some of these small plates. The fried anchovies sound nice and maybe this cheese platter?" I say

"Ooo I want olives too. And some bread." She says laughing with excitement. She looks adorable right now. Right before leaving the van she pulled on her favorite wrap and her dark curly hair is fanned out across her shoulders.

Our server appears from inside the castle. She is in her late twenties with platinum blond hair and big hoop earrings. From a distance she's the kind of person we usually avoid but as she approaches our table a certain confidence and intelligence permeates from her facade.

"Hi guys, my name's Amber and I'm going to walk you through our wines today. Can I get you any food to pair with the wine?" She asks gently.

"Yes, definitely. We'll take the anchovies, olives and cheese plate please." I say.

"Sounds great. I'll put that in for you and get you started right away." She says and turning on her heel hurries back inside. Moments later the speakers turn on to play some light jazz and the scene is now set. We smile at each other with anticipation and excitement. Just to be free and on the road, doing this. A sense of pure joy lights up our eyes.

A few minutes pass and Amber returns with the hostess carrying two glasses and a bottle of wine in one hand and a plate of olives and bread in the other. She expertly places the glasses and bottle down in front of us and begins to pour a healthy taste in each glass.

"Ok so this first wine is our prize winning Chardonnay, the Amor Fati. The art work on each of our bottles is hand drawn by a local artist and the owner of the vineyard. It has really lovely notes of lemon and creme brûlée." She says in one breath. You can tell she's a skilled server because she leaves us in peace to savor the wine and olives. Although only a few sips, each mouthful brings a surprising melody of flavors. You can taste the tart citrus but with a really pleasant and well rounded flavor of the creme brûlée coming through. It's not as oaky as the Chardonnay's that we were used to, which is nice. Swirling the wine in our glasses we try to pretend like we know anything about wine. We must have looked ridiculous while holding our pinkies out in mock refinement. Sometimes it's fun to pretend.

"It's good but I want to try these reds." She says with her chin lifted high.

"Yeah, it's good. I can definitely taste the creme brûlée." I say in my best British drawl.

"You do? Because I don't at all. I think that's just made up." She says laughing.

"I just think it tastes like grapes." She says again. And she's probably right. I have no idea if it actually tastes like the French dessert. I just know it tastes light and refreshing and makes these olives taste amazing. Amber returns carrying another bottle, this time a red.

"Ok, so this is our Pinot Noir. Stasis. It's a well rounded and easy to drink wine that's grown just in the valley." She says while heavily pouring the tastings into our empty glasses.

"What did you guys think of the Amor Fati?" She asks.

"I thought it was great, but she can't taste the creme brûlée." I say while pointing my finger at Sara in mock disgust.

"That's ok honey." And then she leans in and whispers. "The truth is, I can't either."

We all laugh and she leaves us, this time with the fried anchovies in a little ceramic bowl drizzled with olive oil.

"I can't believe you told on me. This Pinot is amazing though." She says after taking a sip.

And she's right. It is amazing. A very smooth and well balanced red that just sort of glides over your tongue, washing the salty fishiness of the anchovies down. We had learned to love these tiny little sea monsters months before at an Italian restaurant and they were perfect with the wine. Amber re-emerges with the last of the bottles to taste and pours an even larger helping of another red.

"This is our Grenache. It's my personal favorite and a real treat with the cheeses." As soon as she speaks the hostess arrives with our small cheese board.

"While we have you here, do you have any other favorite vineyards you'd recommend? We're headed back towards the coast but we have time for a couple more before stopping for the night." I ask, eager to hear a locals perspective.

"Absolutely. If you're headed back towards the coast you've got to stop at Oso Libre. It's my favorite vineyard in the area. My husband and I go every other weekend. And then, if you're headed to the coast you should check out the Hearst Castle tasting room. You can grab a glass of wine and sit right on the water for sunset." She says with confidence. Just the way she says it sets an excited fire in our bellies. She turns to leave and we finish the small cheese board and Grenache wine.

"This is my favorite so far I think. I've actually never tried something like this." I am impressed with the silky smooth texture and rich velvety chocolate flavors.

"Yeah, let's get a bottle of this." She confirms. We linger for a moment longer to buy a bottle of the Grenache and to thank our host. As gaudy as the castle looked, it still had a sense of magic to it. The service industry is another career field that is on its last legs, a great big bloated sea beast rotting slowly on a polluted shore. Most places these days would rather sneer at you then offer a modicum of friendly service. But it was good here. Pleasant and unpretentious. The way Amber moved and spoke was inspiring. You could tell she liked her job. Or at least knew a lot about it. I wondered about her life. She probably lived in a cute cottage somewhere in these hills. A collection of art, probably pastel. A ton of good wine stored away. Maybe some potted plants. I had always hated the service industry but she made it seem elegant and intelligent. I was always a lazy server. Never wanting to meet the eyes of a guest out of fear that they'd linger long enough to try and get to know me. I've worked in a ton of dive bars and shitty restaurants over the years and I can tell you for a fact that we servers hate anyone who walks through our establishments doors, equally and on time.

"It must be a pretty decent gig, working at one of these tasting rooms." I say. She looks over at me and smiles but then shakes her head and says, " I guess. I bet you still get a few pompous assholes. You'd hate it in a week." She's probably right, I think. Looking back and watching the staff runaround de-crumbing, cleaning, taking orders from arrogant hipsters from Los Angeles. A shudder ran up my spine.

Laughing we wave goodbye to the castle and continue down the road towards the right turn that will take us to Oso Libre and the coast. After a few glasses at Tooth and Nail were both feeling pretty cozy cruising down the winding two lane roads. Almost no one is out at this time in the afternoon and it's important we don't speed or take it too fast so we just kind of coast. Sara puts on an old favorite album and we kind of just bop on down the road in our big marshmallow. The instructions she gave us were clear. Turn right and then follow the road through the oak forested hills until you pass through a tree tunnel. After the tunnel you'll see the sign on the left for Oso Libre. Probably takes about fifteen minutes, she had said. And she was right. Just enough time for the tape to reach the end of the first side and turn down the narrow driveway, through the oak trees and a small farm towards Oso Libre. It's probably the most unassuming vineyard we have ever been to. There aren't any fancy gables or signs or fountains and statues that light the way. It's just a farm road and a narrow parking lot. You see the rows of vines and the humble tasting room only after you've pulled into the lot. Looking down the sloped hill to where the vineyard sits you see a dozen or more cows grazing, which is unique in my limited experience with vineyards. The hostess immediately greets us and guides us to a small table looking out over the vineyard.

Our first wine is a crisp Chardonnay. At first it's nothing to write home about in comparison with some of the vineyards further north but after the second sip you can really start to enjoy it. The service here is as good as Tooth and Nail and the wine is flowing. It's not long before a second vintage is poured and then a third. A quick visit from the master vintner and he explains that they've raised organic grass fed beef since the beginning of the winery and that if we'd like we can purchase some in the adjoining shop. The last glass of wine is the bottle we purchase. It's a 2006 Primitivo grown lovingly in the limestone hills that we are sitting on. It's silky smooth and decadent. Like dark chocolate that comes straight from the source. Each small sip is divine and we can't wait to buy a bottle.

"Should we grab some steak to cook over the fire at the campground tonight?" I ask.

"Sure why not, by the time we get down to the coast it will be too late to go to the store." She says, with flushed cheeks and a smile.

Heading into the shop we make our way straight to the beef. It's displayed in neat little packages and expensive, even for the smallest chunk. We shrug and revel in our newly acquired riches. Who needs to be responsible when you have the road to freedom just ahead of you. Let's live in this moment and not be afraid to enjoy the finer things that only kings and emperors and business moguls indulge in. Yes we are tired of being ragged and broken but maybe the wine and steak will make us whole again. We grab two of the nicest looking rib eye steaks we've ever seen and make our way back to the Marshmallow van.

In moments we are rumbling down the farm road and back to the two lane highway with the tunnel of old oak trees and its Zoom Zoom and we're off. No time to waste now, it's late afternoon and we don't want to miss the sunset at the tasting room of Hearst Castle. According to the map, it's not too far. Just need to get back to the highway. Yep, there's the highway sign! Sara is pointing and jabbering and frothing at the bit to get down to the ocean. We've been inland too long now and she wants her sea legs back. Having grown up in New York she craves the sea, it is deep in her Sicilian bones and she will never love me as much as she loves the sea.

The van is moving at improbable speeds now. As if a pointy eared Vulcan is operating the tiller. We're at warp nine and praying that the local fuzz doesn't ensnare us in their speed traps. Passing through the limestone hills we finally come to the very top and before us, facing west is the great expansive Pacific Ocean. Just as we had left it that morning. Looking both gentle and diabolical all at once. In moments we've plummeted down the hill and back towards our beloved Highway 1. Our mobile home is starting to feel tired, as if we've pushed her too hard today. On our right as we pass through the sleepy village of San Simeon we pass the state park where we will be staying the night. It looks uncrowded and we continue on to make the sunset at Hearst tasting room.

Just past San Simeon now and we see the tasting room and pull into a very quiet parking area. We're still giddy from Oso Libre and we nearly skip into the tasting room. They give us a card with a number on it and we make our way outside to a gorgeous outside patio area that is literally right on the shore. The oranges and reds of the sunset are just starting to show their colors against the puffy clouds that have rested overhead all day. We pick a picnic table to nestle into while we wait for our wine samples. It's the perfect little crescent shaped bay that we're looking out onto and the wine flights that arrive glow against the setting sun. We sip our wine and sit quietly, just enjoying each other and the scenery.

"Do you think we could always live like this?" She asks while gazing out at her beloved ocean.

"I'd like to think that's possible. Eventually we'll have to go back to work though." I say.

"Ugh don't say that, let's just try and pretend that this moment will last and that we'll never be sad again and that we will love each other forever."

"We can pretend for now."

"I don't want to pretend. I want it to be real."

"What will we do when the money runs out?"

"We'll just make some more."

"I wish it was that easy."

The last rays of the sun are slowly dropping beneath the distant waves and the light that falls on her face is so perfect and beautiful that she almost resembles the Madonna that hung so delicately in the San Juan Bautista mission. I want her to be happy and for this moment to last forever but I know that it won't. This little adventure will end and winter will turn to spring and summer and eventually we will need to make a decision on what direction we should take in our lives. I look down at my hands and know their potential but I feel more lost than ever not knowing what to do with them. She can tell that I'm struggling so she gets up and sits next to me, snuggling in and resting her head on my shoulder.

"It's going to be ok. We will make it happen."

"Do you promise?"

"I promise."

The sun is now just a sliver of light and in its final moment sends a small green flash across the bay as it disappears for the night. We finish our last sip of wine and walk hand in hand back to the van. All of the other vehicles are gone now, except for the employees and were ready for a good night's sleep. Heading back to the campground we forget about the steak and save it for tomorrow. It's time for sleep and to try and contain our momentary paradise for as long as possible. We drift off quickly after climbing into bed. My dreams come fast and we are still on the road in them and in that fantasy we are happy and in love forever and no one can ever take that away.

Chapter 13

It All Goes to Hell and Then it Doesn't

The morning found us wrapped up together like a pretzel. The cabin was damp and frigid. Like a cold blanket had been set on us in the middle of the night. Moving an inch from our settled positions would spell certain doom. Both of our heads under the covers and Sara's little button nose as cold as ice. The gray light of morning seeping through our sheets woke us slowly like an eroding canyon's walls. First our feet then our knees and then finally our torsos and head slithering out of bed towards the cabin floor. My head was screaming at me. Why? Why would you do this to me? You horrible little man. There are few worse things than a red wine hangover.

"My head feels like a rhinoceros sat on it." I say while groaning and throwing on a hoodie.

"Please don't talk anymore. I hate your voice right now." She says while chuckling at her own struggle. We moved like robots after that. Dressing quickly and starting the engine to warm up the van. Shivering in our seats with the heater blasting, slowly warming the air and our heads throbbing and my gut beginning to find new reasons to hate me. We needed coffee and sugar. A single word wouldn't be spoken until that lofty goal was reached. So before the van even had five minutes to warm up we were once again racing down the Pacific Coast Highway towards the main strip of San Simeon. Just like many of the small hamlets dotting the California coastline if you blink you may miss it. Within a minute we were parking outside of a Mexican restaurant that was open for breakfast. Its flamboyantly colorful exterior perfectly matched the interior and after being quietly ushered to a booth we fell into it like sacks of rotten potatoes. A steaming pot of coffee was brought to the table and our mugs filled. Gingerly sipping the scalding coffee our heads began to clear. The menu was opened and eggs ranchero and steak and eggs were ordered. A bowl of fresh salsa and chips arrived before the food and we wordlessly devoured every bite.

"Wow, I feel a lot better. So, what's the plan?" She asks after stuffing the last chip in her mouth. I unfold the map of the central coast in front of us and trace my finger down the highway.

"We'll make it to Pismo Beach within an hour. I used to go there every summer with my parents and grandmother. I'd love to walk around for a bit. Then maybe we'll keep going after lunch to Santa Barbara for the night." I say between mouthfuls of steak and eggs and salsa and coffee.

"Sounds good to me. No wine for me today." She says laughing. We pay our bill and head back to the van feeling replenished and alive again. We pop a tape in the deck and head down the coastal highway. This part of the road is almost always adjacent to the water and it's gorgeous the whole way. I realize as we are driving that this is where my ancestors one hundred and fifty years ago settled to raise cattle and livestock after a perilous covered wagon journey from the southern United States. Now that's an adventure, I think. Can you imagine settling in the 1800s on the central coast of California? What a paradise. And why did they leave? Imagine owning a hundred plus acres of coastal property now.

We're only about sixty miles to Pismo and we're soon in Morro Bay. Past the campground and then finally to where Morro rock juts out of the water like an eroded fist. We're headed inland now towards San Luis Obispo. Another stop along the Camino Real where the ancient monks had built a bastion of civilization amongst the savage locals. Savages that mostly got along, had little disease and spent their days playing in the surf. But also managed to be riddled with sexually transmitted diseases. Not a bad life. Fishing, sex and the sea. Let's go.

The highway is quiet. It's a Tuesday and past ten o'clock so people are probably at work. I'm hoping that the pier won't be super crowded this time of year. The summer months are almost unbearably saturated in human swarms coming down from the scalding hot interior of the state. San Luis Obispo is another quick blip on the map, we wouldn't be stopping here and we're now headed through the valley and back towards the coast again. The hills lining either side of the road are verdant and green even in these winter months. White washed Spanish style architecture reminds you of the centuries of Latin culture permeating the area.

We passed a sign for Pismo Beach and I can recall the ancient feeling of arriving after being in a slow moving family vehicle, with my little brother and I stuffed in the back seat. The promise of beach time and the arcade always filled me with excitement and I couldn't wait to be far away from my parents and pestering little brother. Entering the city and you can tell that its foundation is built on tourism. It has that classic Route 66 look with big old fashioned signs advertising cold beer and hamburgers. Surf shops and clothing stores and tourist traps line the street. Traffic has picked up slightly but it's still not bad and we quickly find our way to a parking spot along a side street.

"It's not as crowded as I thought it would be. But let's wait and see how the pier looks." I say hesitantly. At any moment a misguided mob of starving tourists could overrun our position.

California is like that sometimes. It can be savage. The walk down to the pier is short as we're only a block or two away. There's a spattering of tourists here and there. Most of them are following our idea of the Pier but it's early and no one is in much of a hurry. These were the same sidewalks that were once wooden and full of teenagers skateboarding and hauling their surfboards to the beach when I was a kid. My brother and I would carry our surfboards and skimboards down to the water and play until we were sunburned and starving.

The big red PISMO BEACH sign is catching a bit of a crowd. People anxious to have their moment in front of the sign for a picture seem to not notice the dozen or so other people wanting to do the same thing. The pier is long and has a few food carts along its path. Nothing is open though. The odd fisherman winds up a cast and sends the line soaring, searching for sculpin or whatever they might get lucky with. A man on stilts walks up and down the pier hoping for a tourist to request an overpriced picture. All in all it's uneventful and almost boring. As a kid I remember it being the most exciting place in California, but now it just seems like an old dream that is never as good as the first time.

"So this is where you used to vacation with your family?" She asks vaguely. I can see that the charm is lost on her. It could also be the hangover but I'm nervous to show her one of my sacred places. I want her to really love it like I did. We look around for a bit longer. Gazing back towards the town and the long stretch of golden sand that meanders further down the coast. The waves are breaking slowly today. Long and clean lines. A few surfers are taking advantage of the empty waves and it's fun to watch them carve their way down the face of the wave. I need to use that board soon, I think. It's been way too long since I was last on a surfboard. Surfing is something that the mind can never forget. It's very easy for the body to lose its connection. We lose our timing and struggle on the first few waves but persistence always brings us back. We walked back towards the van and because we had just eaten breakfast it seemed like it would be a struggle to shovel anymore food down our tumultuous stomachs. Might as well make it to Santa Barbara early and we can set up our camp properly. Getting in the van I take one last look around at all of my childhood memories and turn the key to start the car.

It turns but there's no reaction. I turn it again and a dead, clicking sound. CLICK. CLICK.CLICK.

"Um what's happening, why isn't the car starting?" Sara asks with panic in her voice.

"I don't know, It won't turn over. Did we leave a light on? Is the battery dead?" I say, equally as concerned. We check all of the gauges and indicators. I jump out of the vehicle to pop the hood to see if the battery has been loosened. Everything seems fine, or as far as I can tell. There isn't anything on fire this time. Closing the hood with a bang and I plop back in the driver's seat defeated for a moment.

"It's going to be ok. Maybe we just need a jump. I'll call AAA and we will be back on the road in no time." I say with false confidence. Sara glances over at me with a scarred look. She's been here before when we lost everything only a couple hundred miles ago. All of the weeks of strength and courage start to slip from her features at the possibility of our new home being broken. This can't be happening I think. I walk up the street to a payphone and call the number on the back of my card. I'm thankful for the thousandth time for Aldon. He had forced me to sign up for triple A before leaving. In true dad fashion he refused to ever travel without it. The number connects me to a tow truck service for a jump and it should only be a few minutes, the operator says. I walk back to the van and Sara is outside and under the hood doing her own inspection.

"Do you see anything?" I ask as I approach her looking under the hood. "No and I don't even know what I'm supposed to be looking for." She says with eyes searching the engine block. The panic has left her proud face and now she's just angry and frustrated and hungover.

"The tow truck driver should be here in fifteen minutes. They'll give us a jump and we'll be on our way." I say confidently. Time seems to slow down and I'm gripping the wheel waiting for the driver. What seems like an hour passes and finally the hulking shape of the tow truck lumbers past us and pulls in front. A short and stubby man jumps out and waddles over to us. I get out and greet him and we pop the hood. He looks it over and connects his jumper cables that are attached to a portable battery.

"Ok, let it charge for a minute and then get in and turn over the engine. See if it starts." He says through a week old stubble and tired eyes. I jump back in and wait for him to signal and then I turn the key,

Tick, tick, tick......

"What does this mean?" I asked the man. He can see that I'm desperate but he just shrugs.

"I don't know. I'm not a mechanic. I can take your van to one though." He says with disinterest. He steps away from the vehicle to give us a moment to talk it over.

"What does this mean? Please don't tell me the van is already broken." She says desperately.

"Let's have it towed to the shop. We have money. It will be ok this time." I say confidently.

"Ok, let's get her towed to the shop. Do you know of a cheap one?" I ask with a nervous laugh. He just looks at me with a bored expression and shrugs his shoulders. In moments he expertly hooks up the van and pops her into neutral. We follow him to his truck and climb in. It's cluttered with fast food containers, empty energy drinks and a giant big gulp sits in the cup holder. We sit quietly while he navigates through downtown. In just a few minutes we were at the small shop that's tucked between a bar and a surf shop. The driver nods at one of the employees and it's clear that he knows these people. He probably gets a cut. I'm bitter now because our perfect paradise has been spoiled again and I'm uncertain of what the diagnosis will be. We hop out and talk to the man with a clipboard.

"We can take the van but it won't be until tomorrow or the next day that we can fix it. Sounds like it could be the alternator and we'd need to order a part." He says in a non committal tone. As if to say, do what you want but this is what you're going to get.

"Ok, I guess that's just what we have to do. Can we spend the night in the van? We're sort of on a road trip." I ask. He looks at me incredulously and laughs. "No, you can not stay in your van." He walks away shaking his head. Sara looks at me for direction and it's either going to be miserable or we can make lemonade.

"It's going to be ok. We're just going to have to get a hotel for a couple nights. Let's make this fun. When was the last time we slept in an actual room?" I say to Sara who looks suspicious of everything. Now that I've said that out loud I'm actually kind of excited for a hotel. Maybe we'll even go out to dinner. Not exactly saving money here but for now we can afford this.

"Ok, grab some clothes for both of us and a couple bottles of wine and maybe the Chartreuse. I'm going to go and get details." I say. Trotting over to the office the tow truck driver and the mechanic are looking at me with dead eyes, waiting for the verdict. I walk in with a smile that could light the darkness and say, "Let's do it, we'll stay in a hotel somewhere. How much do you think this will cost?" The mechanic shuffles his feet a bit and after a moment looking at his clipboard says, "It's hard to say. If it's the alternator it shouldn't be too bad. Probably a few hundred bucks." That isn't the worst outcome I think and hand him the keys and sign a few papers. He tells me to give him a call tomorrow afternoon and I head back to the woman and our home.

"It's probably going to cost a few hundred but that's not too bad. We just need to find a hotel now. Maybe we should also get a cocktail at that bar and ask if they know of a good one." I say as we saunter over towards the bar. The building is a squat nondescript shack with just one small neon sign that says, "Drinks". Perfect. Dive bars are the beacons of most civilized society. The door opens and a little bell rings as we enter. It's what we expected. Stepping inside you can immediately smell the cheap booze and cigarettes. Lots of weird wooden carvings and several fake shrunken heads and coconuts line the shelf space above the bar. Being dimly lit we can only make out a handful of day drinkers scattered amongst the long bar. This is where daytime strippers come for lunch break. Taking a seat somewhere in the middle we wait for the bartender.

Emerging from the back room she strides towards us with a big California smile. From a distance she looks like one of those fresh faced college cheerleaders. She's wearing shorts and a tight fitting shirt and her tan skin is dark against the fabric. In the dim light she looks like a femme fatale that you would see in the old noir movies. She is shrouded in mystery until she approaches and you start to see the crevices and you hear her voice croaking behind too many cigarettes. She's perfect for the setting and our dour vibe seems to bring her to us like a moth to flame.

"Hi guys. Welcome to Dave's Tiki Hut. What can I get you?" She rasps and gesticulates towards the tower of booze.

"Two Mai Tais if you can?" I ask and without a word she turns and starts to shake and muddle the fruit. We settle into our stools and look around. The tiki decor is starting to reveal itself in the little nooks and crannies of the bar. A broken surfboard here and a fishing net there. An old pirate of a patron is sitting at a small round table in the back nursing a tall, fruity cocktail. Another ancient couple is tucked into the end of the bar drinking beers and watching a game on the television. It's a cozy little place and off the beaten track which is something we love. It's like a feeling of discovery when you stumble onto anything that's original. It's so rare to find something that has its own voice. Our bedraggled surfer girl is shaking her concoction in a silver bullet and then with skill and finesse she evenly pours our drinks between two rocks glasses with a half lime wedge, fresh mint and a cherry. The drink goes down beautifully. Smooth and tender, like your first sunset over the Pacific Ocean. A perfect pairing of rum, citrus and almond syrup. The bouquet of the fresh mint goes straight to my addled brain stem and begins to heal it with intoxicating power.

"So where are you guys from?" She asks.

"Is it that obvious?" I ask laughing.

"A little bit. Mostly just locals drink here."

"Our van broke down. We're on our way to Mexico. Any chance you know a good hotel nearby?"

"Depends on what you want to spend. The Kon Tiki has good rates now because it's the off season." She says while hurrying over to a regular with an empty glass. After pouring him a beer they lean and whisper in each other's ear. He has the look of a sun-dried tomato with a tuft of bleach blond hair in short spikes. The mai tais are nearly all gone by the time she returns. Without asking she just starts making a new round of drinks in front of us.

"I think you guys need another drink, this one is on the guy at the end of the bar." She says with a laugh in her voice. We look over and the man puts up a quick wave and gets off his stool and saunters over. His face is a cheshire grin and he moves like an animation from the twenties. Steamboat Willie but with a bright floral Hawaiian shirt and two gleaming gold teeth that shine in the dim light of the bar. He lifts his glass to cheers' us and we clink our drinks together.

"I hear your car broke down and you're headed south. That's a shame. But don't worry. People get stuck here all the time. They come in from the interior and when they arrive at the coast something changes. It's the magic that's still here from the old days." He says in a long surfer drawl. "Hey, it's not a bad place to be stuck. The hotel Kon Tiki is a great spot. Full view of the ocean, it's a nice relaxing place. I own a little shop downtown. All kinds of odds and ends. Right next to the donut shop on the main strip. Come by tomorrow and see me if you're still in town." His face breaks into that same cheshire grin, like were edible arrangements or a late afternoon snack. His eyes are a dead gray deeply set against a tanned forehead and bleached spiked hair. His words are almost oily. This is a man who has something to sell.

"Aw thanks man. We appreciate the advice. We'll have to check it out. Right now we need to get into that hotel and figure out our day. Thanks for the drink." I say quickly. Sara looks at me with knowing eyes and we down the drinks and head towards the door. The bartender waves goodbye and the greasy shop owner flashes us another smile.

We can feel the eyes burning holes into our backs as we push open the door into the outside world. We've had too many negative experiences to be roped into whatever that guy is selling, I think. Moments later we were walking up the hill where the bartender had said the hotel was. Now that we're on the southern central coast the weather seems to have warmed up a bit. Only a few scattered clouds in the sky and after the two cocktails our wine hangover seems to be on the mend. Walking hand in hand up the highway we see the retro sign for the Kon Tiki Inn from half a mile away. A massive, half moon shaped building with five stories and an unimpeded view of the Pacific. There's no way this is going to be affordable. It has to be three hundred a night. Crossing the road and making our way through the mostly empty parking lot and I'm hoping for an off season discount. Otherwise it's the motel six at the other end of town.

"Wow, that looks expensive. We need to be careful. The van is already costing us." I say with a nervous edge in my voice.

"Yeah but if it's even a hundred and fifty a night let's take it. I wouldn't mind something nice. It's been a long time since we've slept in a bed that we didn't build." She says excitedly. It makes me happy to see her cheering up. It could be the mai tais talking but it doesn't matter. I'll take what I can get on this one. We walk up to the reception and the door slides open with a silent WHOOSH.

"Hello, welcome to the Kon Tiki. Do you have a reservation?" The lady behind the counter says. She's dressed in professional attire with a little ribbon tied around her neck like a nineteen fifties airline stewardess.

"No reservation. Our van broke down and were just hoping you guys might have an off season deal we can take advantage of?" I say with pleading eyes. I've put on my most charming smile. She looks up and gives us a nod. No emotion. Peering over her glasses. She says. " I think we can do something. Let's see what we have. Do you have AAA?"

"Yes! We actually do." Once again thanking Aldon silently for his foresight.

"Well that will get you ten percent off and if you stay two days I can do it for two hundred total." She says after furiously clicking the keys of her computer like a master pianist.

"Oh wow, ok, yeah I think we'll take it." I say while looking at Sara who is vigorously nodding and smiling. We hand her the cash and she hands us a set of keys with directions to the fourth floor. We grab an ice bucket and fill it full of ice on our way up the white washed stairs. Our massive marshmallow van is parked in between a couple dainty sports-cars and she looks awkward and lonely from the third floor. It takes us seconds to get to our room, taking the stairs two at a time and eager to pour a drink in celebration.

We open the door to reveal a clean and comfortable space, decorated in that Windows 98 color scheme. A perfect king sized bed and a small table with two comfortable arm chairs. The curtains are closed and with one embellished movement I draw them to reveal a balcony that looks directly out to the sea and to the beach below. It's the kind of view that people with good jobs enjoy. In the gardens below there are tall palm trees silhouetted against the blue sky. For a moment we both just stand and stare out at the expanse.

"This is amazing. I can't believe we got it for that price." I say. She turns to look at me and her face breaks into a perfect joyful grin. "I'm actually glad the van broke down now. I think we should celebrate with another drink. A glass of Chartreuse perhaps?" She says laughing. I laugh and reach into the bag to reveal the sultry green liquid. She throws our bags on the bed and slides open the sliding glass door to the balcony. A beautiful warm wind rushes in as I pour the drinks into the glasses packed with ice. My hand slips a little and the glasses are full to the top. The energy in the room is electric and we're ready for the day to truly begin. After spending the last four months living in a van or in a tent, this was paradise. Rooms like this invoke the feeling of stability and normalcy. A man could feel like he has a 401k in a room like this. Maybe even dental.

Our glasses clink and soon the viscous liquid is moving down our throats to mai tai filled stomachs. BAM! WAM! ZAM! Electricity is coming out of our fingertips now as we laugh and skip around the room. Our bare feet sinking into the plush carpet. Sara breaks out the bluetooth speaker and we connect it to the iPod. Soon the room is full of music and laughter and stability. Even if it is only for two nights.

Outside the waves are crashing in long perfect breakers that stretch the length of the beach and Sara is getting dressed to go out for the evening. I can't help but stare at those endless breakers. I had dreamt of surfing for what seemed like years now. Before making our way back west and living in New York where the waves were made of concrete and scattered rubbish, I had lived in Hawaii on the island of Kauai.

I had met Sara at a campground in Hanalei when we were both new and fresh in the world. To save money we camped on a secret beach and would hike out to our jobs in the village. Life was so pure you could drink it. I had a used surf board with holes and dings but I still paddled out. The warm water and the perfect slice that a board makes when you drop into the wave. Fresh fruit grew all around us and we starved and had fires on the beach under perfect starry nights with the waves crashing and the fire snapping. Coconuts and first kisses. Holding hands while we stood ankle deep in the perfect golden sand watching a fiery sunset and trying to keep hair out of our eyes. We were just at the very beginning of getting lost and chasing after the magic.

※   ※   ※

"What were you just thinking about?" She says while taking my hand and looking up at me.

"Kauai and surfing and you." I say while looking back down at her. "I don't remember feeling this concerned about what was next then. Do you?" I ask.

"No. We didn't care at all. I'd love to go back to that feeling." She says dreamily. "What I really want right now is that teriyaki burger from Hanalei. What was it called?" She asks while releasing my hand and turning back to putting on her makeup in the mirror.

"Bubbas Burgers. I'm half starved just thinking of it."

"Oh my god, yes! Bubbas. It was the first meat I had eaten in almost ten years. I was never a vegetarian again after that." She says laughing.

"I need food. Let's get into town and find something to eat. Maybe even a teriyaki burger." I say while hurrying to get dressed.

I quickly throw on a pair of board shorts and my best aloha shirt that's only slightly wrinkled. She's in her black polka dotted dress that reveals her perfect shoulders. I think about how lovely she looks when she's happy and the electricity returns. It courses through my veins and out the top of my head and fingertips.

Moments later we are back to walking down the street towards the pier. We were in a different realm now. Transported far away, to a distant shore. Where the drums beat into the inky black darkness of an endless horizon. Color, sounds, taste, all were heightened and exploding with the magic.

Skipping down the road with the ocean on our right and the mountains on our left. The road runs straight into downtown where all of the cafes, bars, surf shops and restaurants are packed in a comfortable square half mile or so. It's actually getting busier and the traffic of gongoozlers and inner state refugees are flooding the street chaotically. People forget themselves when they are on vacation.

All of us, individually, are the main characters of our own stories. We forget that anyone else exists. Even the best of people will turn into beasts on vacation. And that's why navigating through crowds of tourists can be a bloody engagement. One must know the way. Today though, it didn't matter. We were high on the electric current. Loving every second of the madness. Dodging the families walking five deep along the busy sidewalk, shoving people out of their way like westward expansion.

The smell of good food and the sea permeated the crowded boulevard. As we neared the pier we found a nice two story restaurant with rooftop seating and a full bar. As soon as we had left the swarm of humans moving and groaning their way to the water we felt a huge sense of relief. The air felt different even. Gone was the smell of cheap perfume and suntan lotion. The darkened waiting area had a few scattered people waiting but with the magic all around us we were able to get a table quickly. The teenage hostess took us upstairs and sat us at a table that had a clear view of the pier. We settled in to look at the menu and enjoyed our perch above the hordes of the living dead.

"I did not expect the city to be that busy after how quiet it was this morning." She said, clearly exasperated after navigating through the crowds. "Yeah that was unexpected. I knew it got busy in the summer but this is the off season. Must be some kind of holiday that we don't know about."

"It's Valentine's day. Everyone comes in from LA and the Central Valley." Says a waiter who just appeared from behind a divider that was covered in potted plants and flowers. "Can I get you guys anything to drink?" He asks while holding a notepad and leaning on one hip. A look of pure boredom and disdain oozes from this man. I'd imagine he would look exactly the same way if an asteroid was hurtling towards earth. Just sick of our shit and ready for it all to be over.

"Two Mai Tais please and two teriyaki burgers with fries and a side of ranch." The waiter rolls his eyes and jots everything down half heartedly and turns quickly away to help the next unsuspecting table.

"Oh shit, he's right it's Valentine's day. I had completely forgotten." She says laughing. Hallmark holidays never really integrated into our relationship. In the last three years we had rarely bought each other a gift outside of Christmas. The idea of it all just seemed so disingenuous. Forced even. My stomach growled with anticipation. Breakfast was hours ago and the good booze and all the excitement were making me hungry.

The teriyaki burgers were a sign that we were in the right place and when the drinks came out our buzz came flooding back. The burgers weren't exactly Bubbas in Kauai but they did the trick and we were soon skipping about the town and ready for the next pulse of electricity. We had forgotten about the van and its troubles. We had forgotten about the road ahead and all of our unanswered questions. It was back to that clean and pure energy where we were just us without any reservations. Flitting through the mob didn't seem as bad now as we hopped from bar to bar. The tiki theme continued throughout the early afternoon.

We were really flying by the time we got down to the pier. Deciding to go back to the hotel we made our way down to the sand and followed the beach towards the staircase at the back of the hotel. Walking hand in hand we took our time. Clouds had begun to roll in over the horizon and the light shifted to an almost sepia tone. Our feet and toes digging into the sand and the gentle waves expanding and contracting around us.

"You know, I really love you."

"You do?"
"Oh yes. Happy Valentine's day my love."
"Happy Valentine's day."

Chapter 14

Riding the Cosmic Wave

The stretch of highway that runs from Pismo beach to Santa Barbara veers inland for a short while, passing through the little tourist town of Solvang.

Years ago when the waves of immigrants were pouring into the San Ynez Valley, a group of Danish farmers founded the town and built the small city that you see today. Its architecture brings you back to the old world with its post and beam construction and charming European facades. We didn't have time to stop but it's worth noting that it would easily be a place we could have spent several days exploring. Pismo beach had been a grand distraction and when the van was all fixed up we were ready to get back on the road. Mexico was calling and although we still had money it was quickly being drained by our recent activities. The van was a simple fix and now that we were back on the road there was a renewed sense of purpose.

Santa Barbara, for me, is an almost mythological city. It was where my parents had lived and gone to university and countless small trips up the coast found us there. It is the first truly quintessential California city, if you're coming down the coast from San Francisco. Tall palm trees wave at you from perfect golden sand. White washed Spanish architecture and palm trees saturate the city and some of the most beautiful, relaxed humans on earth call this area home. You definitely need a six figure income though. Good luck if you're living out of your van. If you thought Northern California frowned on transients...

Our newly repaired marshmallow cruised through the city at a steady sixty five. This would have to be another place to return to someday I thought as we cranked up the radio and focused on the drive. It was still early and if we were lucky we'd beat the manic state of panic that is Los Angeles rush hour traffic. Few places will bring a shudder up my spine as the memory of countless hours spent in the accordion of terror. If you ever thought that tourists on foot could be anymore horrible all you have to do is spend six hours in LA traffic.

Our little mobile home is cruising now. Whizzing past Ventura and all of those ancient memories of the fairgrounds come dancing back. Fried food and rides, maybe a kiss from a stranger. Sara is rummaging in the back seat for a snack and I'm just trying to focus on not getting us killed as the maniacal city folk wiz past me. The road is right on the ocean now and the weather is getting warmer with every mile.

"Oh Shit." I hear Sara say in the back.

"What? Is everything ok? What's wrong?" I say, panicking for a moment. She scurries up to the front trying to stay on both feet as the van lurches around while we drive the marshmallow at a thousand miles an hour. She's holding a package of something and a deep frown creases her soft face.

"We forgot to eat the steak." She says, holding the package up to be inspected after settling in her seat.

"Is it still good? Open it up and smell it. It was in the cooler right?" I ask half paying attention to the road but hoping that those perfect steaks still have some life in them. "They look ok actually, they don't smell at all. The cooler was still pretty cold the whole time even though the ice melted." She says victoriously. Through all of the drama and celebrations of the last couple days we had completely forgotten the epic bottles of wine and the steaks we had purchased at Oso Libre.

"We'll have to cook them this afternoon when we find a campground for the night. First I need to get through this insane traffic." I say, while white knuckle gripping the steering wheel and cursing every other car. Why is it that people drive this fast in such sketchy areas? Look at how many cars there are. That motorcyclist literally just took a gamble for what? Three car paces. Slow down people, you're not really saving any time. At this point I'm just trying to hold her steady in the slow lane. The monstrosity of the highway stretches on, clogged with drivers hell bent on an early death.

*   *   *

We've entered the city limits of Santa Monica and it means more city driving. Even the colors are changing as we continue south. Santa Monica is vibrant and full of life. Colorful characters strut down the street with half naked golden vixens so lithe and perfect that they seem straight out of a Baywatch episode. Sprinkled throughout the crowd are some of the sketchiest looking people on planet earth. That guy on roller blades in a speedo is definitely on a sex offender registry somewhere. Our clunky home on wheels rumbles past all of the color and craziness and there's no time to stop. The goal today was to make it to San Clemente in the early afternoon so I could paddle out on a familiar wave. I was desperate to finally get in the water and this stretch of sand from San Clemente to San Diego was my home turf.

I had spent the formative years there, with friends that had long since disappeared from my life, camping and surfing and throwing late night bonfire parties. Lots of mistakes were made in those ancient times. Lots of haywire hormones. Promises that were broken. Crimes committed. Hearts broken. Both mine and theirs. Also those bleach blond tips and sea shell choker necklaces. Don't know what I was thinking there.

The road straightens back out after Santa Monica but the traffic is always there. Even now at around two o'clock in the afternoon on a Tuesday. Aren't you people supposed to be at work? I think as I glance at the car maintaining my speed next to us. He's in a slick Audi sports-car and his chiseled look is full of importance and intent. He definitely has a dental plan, works a fifty hour a week office job and still manages to run marathons and raise children with his beautiful wife Laura and their golden retriever....

"Hey are you paying attention? You need to get over. Our exit is coming up." She says while looking at the map. I've been distracted by the flow of a thousand faces and I shake out of it to begin an aggressive maneuver. "Batten down the hatches and buckle your seatbelts! We're making way!" I cry out like a swarthy sailor with many a year at sea. The marshmallow van swerves violently ahead of a car desperate to close the gap. Not today asshole! Only one more lane to go and there's another car closing in but a quick lurch of the wheel and I'm in. Another driver foiled in his reckless adventures. Sara is gripping her seat in terror and saying a prayer to the virgin and the sweat is pouring down my face but we made it.

San Clemente and the state park where we would stay the night was just ahead. The ocean stretches before us and the waves are looking perfect. Long, even breaks that are maybe shoulder high and the sun is shining. My excitement levels are at their peak now. Our marshmallow home is blasting the local surf rock station and the sign for the campground is already in view.

This time there's no escaping the campground fees as a cheery older woman in a crisp rangers uniform takes my license and information after charging us the fee. Smiling, she points in the direction to our campsite which is right on the sand. It's off season here and there are very few campers and tents as we slowly drive to our spot in the far corner of the site. Easily we see the corner lot, tucked behind a few bushes right next to the beach which slopes down towards the water. Privacy is so key in picking the perfect camp spot. We parked the van with our sliding door facing the ocean and the road completely blocked from view. The early afternoon sun is drifting towards the horizon now and I only have a couple hours left before sunset so with very few words I jump to the back of the van to get into my shorts and wet suit. People mistakenly believe that the water is warm in California. It is not. In fact it's frigid this time of year but in the spring and summer it starts to warm to a reasonable temperature that still makes your nipples hard. Even in July.

Opening up the back doors and pulling out the old board and grabbing the wax from the closet. I start to wax up the board where I'll be attempting to stand. Attempt is the key word here. It's important to make it out before the late afternoon rush. Right now there's only a few surfers scattered in the line up. Considering that I haven't surfed in several years I expected to be rusty. A lot of these locals don't like new surfers taking up prime real estate on their home waves. Things can get dicey if you're not paying attention.

"Ok, I guess I'll just set the whole camp up by myself then?" She says with her hands on her hips and a playful smile. "Yes thank you, that would be great babe." I say, completely distracted by the most recent set of waves. She laughs and swears at me as I trot with the board under my arm towards the ocean. It's an uncrowded beach at this hour with only a few people scattered up and down the coast. The first step into the water and my toes curl up into themselves. Knee deep now and I'm trudging straight to the first small wave that's coming. I belly flop onto my board to ride over it and begin to paddle towards the next small set.

The water isn't as cold as I thought it would be. The wetsuit did its job allowing my body temperature to be insulated enough that after a couple minutes it felt like a comfortable level of cold. Still cold, but refreshing. Like jumping into a fresh lake in the heat of summer. I'm headed towards the center of a break that only has one other person waiting in the line up. Straddling his board he bobs up and down as I flounder my way behind him. First come, first serve is the law of the wave.

I'm worried he will smell my rust from a mile away but he just nods and gets ready to paddle into his set. I straddle my board and look back for the next set as the surfer ahead of me paddled in and popped straight up and began carving up the wave like a roast turkey. Sending back spray over the top of the crest as he rounds the wave and rides it almost all the way to the shore. The next wave comes fast and I lurch forward to catch it, paddling furiously but missing the catch. Remember first learning to drive a stick shift? It's like that. I curse to myself and wait for the next wave to roll in. The surfer has already skillfully started to paddle back to the line up and as he passes me he says, " Hey man don't paddle so fast. Just quick strong pulls and you'll get it. Just got to find your timing bro." He pushes his long blond hair back behind his ears and smiles while gliding behind me.

The next wave has momentum now and builds and builds while lifting us high in the air. I follow his advice and with hard intent dig my open paws into the water and pull. The next moment is bliss as the board catches and glides forward quickly. I push up on the board and pop to my feet, legs placed evenly apart and I'm on the wave! The water glides under my feet like quicksilver and I cut down the face of the wave until I reach the base.

I'm flying now, for just that one second, the wind is in my hair and the beach is coming closer as I speed down the face. In the next second my legs buckle and I fly head over heels back into the water. My face nearly smashes into the sand bar as the tail end of the wave grabs me and forces me into a tumultuous washer machine that tumbles me over and over until my leash tugs me back towards my floating board. I pop back into the world and take a deep breath.

"Wooooo!" I cry out while pumping my fist into the air. I'm back, baby. I quickly look around to see if anyone saw my spectacular one second ride but it's still just me and the other surfer waiting for a decent wave. I start my paddle back towards the line up and smile at him on the way. He laughs a little and shakes his head before turning to catch a mammoth of a wave and continues to rip the wave into shreds. Watching him ride the wave was like watching a skilled craftsman at work. The way he could quickly read the map of the moving water, guiding him up and down to the very crest and back again.

The next wave isn't as big but it's still shoulder high and this time I catch it easily and quickly jump to my feet. My toes facing forward I glide down and reach out a hand to drag behind me against the smooth surface of the wave. Any troubles I had faced before that moment, the traffic, the van breaking down, all of it. It was all gone. I was just completely present. A moment in time, almost flash frozen. That same perfect feeling of the water beneath my feet. And then three seconds later I'm face planting back into the same sandbar and being tossed around like an old sock in a public laundromat. Even the worst wipe out wouldn't melt the fools grin that spread from ear to ear as I popped out of the ocean and paddled with renewed energy back to the lineup. Passing the surfer he looks up and smiles and offers a hang loose and a nod. The ultimate acknowledgement. The waves are speeding up and blowing out before they form rideable waves so I bob up and down waiting. Behind me I can see a massive wave building and for a moment I have "the fear". It's too big. I can't catch that. Looking back towards the other guy and he's waving me on to it. Smiling, the bastard, he's encouraging me onto the wave. Shit. I can't back out now, I'll look like an asshole. Alright let's do this. I forward plop onto my belly and begin to paddle, quick, even strokes until the giant wave grabs me with its mighty paw. I feel the stick and then the catch and I'm popping up to step off into oblivion. The drop looks like its three stories tall and the bottom is surely my doom but just as I might have tumbled into the depths, I lean into the wave and I ride it towards the base, this time though I push my right foot towards the wave and the board carves back up the wall to the center where my head just barely peaks over the crest. The wave is starting to barrel now, not a big stand up barrel but one where I have to crouch down and duck into the spiral suction cup of the cosmos. Nothing in the world comes close to being in a barrel. It has that shiny smooth groove as it lopes over head and tumbles down into the fray. For the next four seconds I squeeze through the barrel until the wave finally consumes me and I go round and round through the tumbler again. Swimming to the surface where my loyal steed awaits, I see the surfer waving over head and giving me two big thumbs up. He catches the next mammoth wave and disappears down the barrel and towards the beach. I lose him then as I paddle back for one more wave. I turn to quickly catch it but it's moving too fast and I just don't make it in time then it blows out sending me spinning through the cosmos once more.

Wading out of the water with the board under my arm and the sun setting I was physically exhausted. My body felt like I had just been trampled by a herd of elephants. Stumbling back towards the van and the campsite I noticed the other surfer taking off his wetsuit. Passing him he waved me over. "Hey bro, looks like you scored a couple decent waves out there." He said with a grin. "Yeah man, I can't believe that last big one. I actually got barreled for the first time in three years." I say excitedly. "Just had to find your timing, that's all. Where are you from?" He asks. "I'm from San Diego but we've been living in New York for the last couple years. Landlocked." I explain. He shrugs and says, " Nothing wrong with that. It's good to see the world. I'm on a road trip myself." He quiets down now and the conversation ends cordially as I nod and stumble back through the soft sand to Sara and the camp.

"Did you see that? I got into a barrel for like four seconds." I say excitedly as I peel off the wetsuit and lean the board against the van.

"I didn't see you get in a barrel, I did see you get destroyed by that last wave though." She says laughing. The camp has been set up perfectly. Secretly she loved to set everything up. It was her way of feeling comfortable. In all of our chaos it was the one thing she could control. I think as long as she had that she'd be ok sailing to the freaking moon. If it was up to me we'd just spread everything out on a blanket for easy access and not be organized at all. She hung up the fairy lights again from a post and the picnic table had a spread of snacks and a cutting board where she was preparing dinner. A glass of wine had been poured and at least half a bottle of a Navarro Pinot Noir dranken.

"Ha, well I see you broke into the good stuff. I might have a glass myself. After all, why not?" I say while hanging up the wetsuit to dry and taking a seat at the table. "That was amazing. It took me a minute to get my timing back but I actually caught a few waves. It felt amazing to be in the water again." I said in an excited tempo. The adrenaline was still pumping through me. Pouring a glass of wine and rolling a joint was needed now. I could taste the salt on my lips and my head still had that glow you sometimes get after a workout. The temperature had dropped just a little and the salt water was making my skin sticky and itchy.

"I'm going to wash this salt off at the outdoor shower near the bathrooms. I'm all itchy." I say while peeling off the rest of the wetsuit. She shrugs and continues to set up for dinner. Trotting over to the bathrooms the surfer was finishing up washing off his wetsuit, looking up he gave me a nod of acknowledgement as I approached. "You guys are camping here too? Nice. How long are you staying?" He asks, stepping away from the shower.

"Probably just tonight. We're headed to Mexico and were pretty eager to make the border before the weekend. Might stay another day in San Diego." I say in one breath. It feels good to meet a fellow traveler and to trade stories.

"Sweet. I'm headed to Mexico as well. And then beyond. Just me and my dog and a few surfboards." He says with a mellow smile. The pace of his voice is slow and soft. Almost as if he's trying to remember a comfortable dream. His whole demeanor is relaxed and poised. His complexion is a deep brown with crinkles at his eyes and the corners of his mouth. Long blond hair, bleached in the sun is pulled back into a small knot at the back of his head. This is a man who has spent his whole life on the water. His smile seems healthy and genuine and his movements are graceful and balanced. I immediately wanted to ask this guy everything. I needed to know who he was.

"Hey we're going to smoke a joint and have a few glasses of wine if you want to join us later at the van? I haven't been to Mexico since I was a kid so if you have any suggestions on quiet little places where the surf is uncrowded and steady I'd love to know...." I say in another long breath while turning on the water and starting to wash the wet suit.

"Ha, doesn't everybody want to know. I go every year. Yeah maybe I'll stop by later. Catch ya." He flashes a peace sign and retreats back towards a van that's parked on the other side of the lot.

Rinsing off the salt water and reflecting on the epic session I had just had, rejuvenated my scattered mind. For a moment on that wave I had lost track of time itself. I could hide there and maybe buy some time before the bigger questions needed to be answered. The air outside was still a pleasant temperature and I could smell the small charcoal grill that Sara had set up. Gingerly walking barefoot across the campsite to our van it suddenly hit me that I was starving. There's something about salt water and meat that provide a marriage of flavor and sense that is unbeatable. When I was a kid my best friend and his dad would sometimes take me out on half day fishing boats in the San Diego bay. I remember Jake's dad saying that there was nothing like a cheeseburger from a galley at sea. The sea air is the best compliment to a burger. And you know something? He was right.

"That BBQ smells amazing. What are we throwing on the grill? I'm starved." I ask after tucking away the washed wet suit in a bag and stuffing it under the bed. Sara is relaxing in one of our folded chairs with a full spread on the table. There were two onions chopped in half, tomatoes ripe from the autumn harvest and a long poblano pepper. The steaks had been taken out of the packaging and placed on our cutting board seasoned with salt and pepper. Everything is just waiting to be scorched with delicious charcoal flavored heat. Two glasses of wine were laid out and a joint rolled. The smile on her face was as smug as a cat after catching a mouse. And I laughed and gave her a kiss on the nose and said, "look at this cornucopia". Reaching into a little pouch behind the front seat I grab a joint and light it up with a cupped hand to protect the flame from a small breeze. I eagerly move towards the grill, grabbing the glass of wine and taking a long deep inhale of the Pinot and the smell of the sea and the good earth. The smell of the sizzling meat and the lit joint were so perfect that it was sad to think of life being any other way.

The sun was just starting to add extra color to the horizon and the sound of the waves echoed off our van. "I invited that guy I met out on the water for a drink later. Seems like an interesting character. He's also headed to Mexico." She's rummaging in the back looking for our speaker to throw on some music. "Ok cool. Only a couple because we need to be on the road for San Diego tomorrow." He didn't look like a big talker and I doubted if he'd even stop by. The steaks were cooked to a perfect medium rare and the veggies grilled. The wine and the grass fed steaks and the sound of the ocean gave us both that special magic that only comes from perfect days. The madness of the traffic was a distant memory and we spent the next couple hours laughing and enjoying our meal and each other.

The sun was just about to blink out of existence when my new friend showed up with a small dog in tow. Carrying a six pack and a shy smile. His clothes were markedly Californian. A clean quicksilver hoodie and a backwards hat along with board shorts and old worn sandals. He approached gingerly. With a shy grin and quiet eyes.

"Hey guys, are you still up for a drink?" He says holding out a beer.

"Yeah man, I'm James and this is Sara. Take a seat!" I say enthusiastically. He moves the bench and takes a seat and cracks open a beer.

" My name is Will and this little rat is called Harry." He says and releases his tiny little terrier. He runs up to Sara wagging his tiny tail begging for food and she hands her some gristle from her plate and drops it to the ground where Harry greedily eats it up in one or two bites.

"So you guys are headed to Mexico? Anywhere in particular?" He asks casually. Crossing his stretched out legs he reaches to take the joint I pass him.

"We're not really sure. Just going to Ensenada first. We'd love to find a less crowded area. Somewhere to take it easy for the rest of winter." I say hoping for a tip or some insight from this wise, older traveling surfer.

"There's a lot of space south of the border. You just need to find it. I know a place you guys could try. The waves aren't always amazing but when they're on they are on. Lots of big waves down that way so definitely get some more experience first." He says in a soft voice. You can tell he's not judging but a feeling of embarrassment reddens my face. I guess my rustiness was more apparent and my four second wave rides were not as impressive as I had thought.

"I grew up surfing. I just need to get back into the routine I think." I say, trying not to sound defensive and a little disappointed at the same time.

"Look, I'm not saying you don't know how to surf. You caught some good waves today. I can just tell you haven't found your timing yet and it's important to be safe when you're in water that fast and big. Today was just barely overhead. Down south in the winter you're looking at some serious waves. Just be careful." He says in his same even tone while taking a sip of beer and passing the joint back.

"Yeah you're totally right. It has been a while. That's why I'd love to find some uncrowded spots. Less annoying to locals." I say. He shrugs and leans back further to scratch his dog's head who has settled behind him in the sand.

"If I were you I'd head west from San Quentin. Go to a place called Puerto Santo Tomas. It takes a while to get there from the highway and there's almost nothing there. Just a shop and a taqueria and a gentle right hand break that should be good for you." He says with an almost nostalgic tone. You can tell he's a man of few words and this is probably the best we're going to get so we spend a few minutes just smoking the joint and enjoying the rest of the sunset against the horizon. His eyes are still roving the surface of the ocean to judge the swell and plan for tomorrow.

"If you want to find the magic, it's there. But if you're not careful it can keep you for a long time. It's very easy to do and if you go you'll see why." He says quietly. His voice is somewhere far away, over the horizon. In a place almost mythical and forbidden. It's obvious the subject is closed now, he's given his advice and if I was paying attention I'd find it. We let silence embrace the conversation for a few minutes while we look out onto the water and relax deeper into the vibe.

"How long have you been surfing?" I ask casually after a spell. He looks over at me slowly and takes a sip of beer. "My entire life. I'm from Santa Cruz. Started when I was a kid and even made it a career for a little while." He says nonchalantly.

"Whoa, you were a pro? That must have been amazing?" I say excitedly. He just gives us a sad smile and lets out a little laugh. "Best thing that ever happened to me and I miss it every day. Life got in the way though. Kids. An injury. Divorce. Old age." He said nostalgically. This time with definite sadness in his voice.

"Were you able to travel much as a pro?" I ask, hoping to bring up a good memory. He turns away for a moment to take one last glance at the darkening sea.

"Oh yeah. All over the world. Tahiti, Portugal, Indo. Lived in Australia for a year." He says while waving his hand in a vague direction.

"That's amazing. Literally a dream life. I'm still trying to figure out a career. It's probably going to have to be something awful like a legal secretary or an insurance salesman. But if I had the ability I'd love to be a pro surfer." I say.

"I don't know man. It's not all it's hyped up to be. The first couple years it's all party and play. Girls, drugs, lots of late night boozers and early morning surf sessions. You're the man when you're twenty and winning. Then someone younger and stronger shows up and changes the game. People come and go. Some die. Some go to jail. It's not as easy as it seems, is what I'm trying to say I guess." He claps his hands and Harry jumps up into his lap and we relax in silence for a while longer.

"What about you Sara? Are you trying to figure out a career?" He asks with a smile. The question shakes Sara out of her gaze towards the dark waters and answers with a confidence that surprises me. She stretches and says,

"No, I don't care about a career. I just want to travel and live life. I'm tired of trying to be normal." Her voice drifts off, drowned by a wave crashing and we go back to a comfortable silence. The sun has officially said goodnight and a few stars emerge, twinkling softly through the ambient light of Los Angeles further north and San Diego to the south.

"Well, maybe I'll catch you guys down in Mexico but I think I'll call it a night. Early start. I think your girl has the right idea. Just go and live. Forget about all of the other stuff." He says, rising and grabbing his last few beers.

"Hey thanks for the tip on Puerto Santo Tomas. And for the tip in the water. Hopefully we'll see you down south." I say reaching out a hand. "Yeah man, nice to meet you guys. I should be down there in a few weeks. Take your time. Enjoy the good life." He says after taking my hand and giving it a strong squeeze.

Disappearing into the night with the little rat dog in tow.

"Interesting guy. I'm down to go to Santo Tomas if you are? Sounds perfect." I say after he's out of earshot. Opening the front door to find the map so we can mark the location I find one of the opened bottles of chartreuse and laugh. "We've definitely met some interesting characters on this trip. Cant believe that guy was a pro surfer. I could see it, he was incredible on the water." I pour two little glasses of Chartreuse and reach down to grab her hand. Leading her towards the beach so we can put our feet in the sand.

"Yeah I'm interested to check out that town. I don't want to forget about La Paz though." She says staring straight ahead at the ocean. She's quietly shuffling her feet and I can tell that something is off.

"What's wrong?"

"I just don't like thinking about finite things. Why do we have to keep talking about careers? I just want to take a chance on the world. That guy was a little spaced out but I think he's right."

"After the car broke down I just seriously started to question all of this. Being homeless wanderers just wasn't big on my list of dreams as a kid." I say tensely.

"Bullshit it wasn't. You've been a traveler for years. We're gypsies and we just need to accept that. We don't need to be homeless. We have the van now." She says defensively. And she's right and it made me angry. I was twenty seven and most of my childhood friends were already settled into a career. I don't think they ever understood me in those years. I was adrift on dangerous currents while they had set an anchor in safe harbors.

"Whoa, are you mad at me for some reason?" I snap back.

"I don't know. I just don't see why we have to keep pretending to be normal to everyone we come across. We are not normal. We're weird, we're broken. Why force this image of what everyone else wants from us?"

"I'm not trying to force anything. I just have this idea of what life is supposed to be and it's hard for me to embrace this lifestyle long term." I say, my voice raising with frustration. Not because what she's saying is wrong but because it's the truth. Nothing hurts more than truth.

"Well, you're wrong. Life isn't supposed to be anything. We're just a blip in the universe. Why do you HAVE to get a career? Why do you HAVE to be normal? Is it so wrong that we just spent the last few months adventuring down a beautiful coastline and had the most original experience of our lives? Do you really want to go back to an office job? Or worse yet a restaurant job?" She says, fuming now and hopped up on the energy of her emotions and maybe a little from the wine and Chartreuse.

"I don't know, maybe you're right. We have seen some pretty amazing things. It's just that everyone I know seems to be doing better than me. They're all settling into their careers. Making the big moves towards a future and here we are. What do we have? Six thousand dollars to our name? It's just been nagging at me." I say quietly. Defeated.

"Just stop. We are right where we are supposed to be. After the car broke down and we were stranded something just clicked in my brain. Then meeting Aldon and Sharon. I have this feeling we're supposed to be doing this. I want to see how far we can go." She says passionately. I've never seen her like this. So committed to a belief. She really feels this way and it's a mighty thing to behold.

"Wow. Yeah maybe you're right. You're actually kind of inspiring right now." I say laughing and breaking the tension.

"Yeah, well, I've got a few tricks up my sleeve you haven't seen yet." She says laughing. She swigs the rest of her Chartreuse and sets the glass in the sand. Standing, she reaches out her hand to lead me towards the water. For awhile we just walk in reach of the gentle waves lapping the shore. The water covers our feet and does its tired best to pull us out to sea. Glittering stars overhead smile down on us with wise and ancient light. They seem to know all of the secret truths. Our footsteps disappear as we wander up the beach and my mind drifts back to the feeling of the sea grabbing me and throwing me back into the cosmos. Maybe she's right. This is life. How could this feeling ever exist in an ordinary world?

Chapter 15

Coming Home

When Juan Rodriguez Cabrillo sailed into the San Diego Harbor his first contact with the locals proved to be amicable. His mission, given to him by Cortez, was to find the mysterious continent of India and claim the land for the glory of Spain. To Cabrillo and his men, the bay was simply a good place to lay anchor. They had no way of knowing the future of the city or the people that lived there. In those days there were no palm trees swaying gently along the promenades. It would be generations before those iconic trees would make their way across the Pacific Ocean. The famous citrus groves and corporate agriculture wouldn't come for centuries. In fact the area would remain uninhabited by Europeans for another two hundred years. The natives would continue in their mostly peaceful existence with no reckoning of the future.

They would have had no way of knowing about the places that I would grow up loving. It would be another four hundred years before the Del Mar fairground was established. How could they have guessed that not far from where they first anchored a typical city street would be transformed into the cultural mecca of the Gas-lamp District. Or that somewhere along the sloping bay a district called Seaport Village would rise up to become a tourist destination for millions of international travelers. The Spanish did not have a clue about a lot of things. And back then their food was not the tapas and paella of the future. It was all gruel and hardtack, moldy bread with a protein boost of fresh maggots. Can you imagine Cabrillo walking down a street and tucking into a taqueria? His clunky metal armor smashing into the salsa bar. Imagine for a moment his wine soaked lips allowing his first al pastor taco to enter his mouth. That first bite. Imagine. I can see him raising his gauntleted fist at the half naked heathens that stroll along the pier and shaking his head at the strange sports being played along the sand. In those early days there was no traffic so how could he understand the pain of two travelers stuck on the I-5, In a gigantic marshmallow jammed in between two gigantic metal vehicles and all around them smaller vehicles screaming by at terrible speeds. It was this way for us as we struggled our way down the interstate. We had hoped to wake up early enough to beat the traffic but apparently a couple thousand other people had the same idea.

The decision had been made to find a camping spot for a couple days just south of Del Mar in Torrey Pines. This was my home turf. I had grown up inland in a smaller city called Poway. A place of no real importance other than the Hamburger Factory, Blink 182 and a few good Mexican restaurants. It was a pretty standard suburban community to grow up in but the moment my friends and I could drive we were away west. To the coast running from La Jolla to Torrey Pines. Here you could find some of the best waves along the California coast. Blacks Beach, swamis, La Jolla shores and the Oceanside Pier. We grew up flailing about trying to find our timing both on the waves and on land. I think all of us, after reaching a certain point of adulthood, would cringe at who we were as teenagers. Probably because of their outdated hairstyles or the neon colors that seemed to permeate the 90's. I have serious reasons to cringe. I was a total weirdo. Not only was I awkwardly shaped with my lanky arms and daddy long legs but I had that common affliction of teenage boys where we think we are better looking than we actually are. I had no fear when it came to talking to girls above my station. I have a distinct memory of handing the cutest girl in my middle school a dozen roses, only to be met with sincere disgust. I was made of more durable stuff then as I just shrugged it off and handed the same discarded roses to another girl, just as cute with pretty much the same reaction. I was desperate for attention. Family life wasn't great and my escape was the romance of classical literature. I would spend my time equally between chores on the ranch, nose in a book, surfing or with my one best friends Jake riding our bikes and exploring the hills of our community. Lots of victories took place in those days. It wasn't all awkward and terrible. Many days of exploration both internal and external.

A now famous and immortalized day when my best friend, two others and I ditched school and roamed our city and one by one were caught by the authorities or our parents. Or the time Jake and I rode our bikes all the way from Poway to Torrey Pines without telling our folks. Our first major venture outside of our known world. We peddled furiously up and down hills and carefully navigated the busy freeway to make it. When we finally arrived we realized that we had made a grave error. We didn't count on having to ride back. It was over twenty miles. We were little. And very tired. When I called my dad he was less than thrilled but agreed to meet us at a Mexican restaurant nearby. Jake and I scratched together enough money in silver coins to buy us both burritos and I can still taste the first bite. So many of these stories take up precious space in my memory and barring any major head trauma I'm sure they will continue to do so. But that was then and this is now. The memory did not change the fact that I was still stuck in gut wrenching traffic and driving a giant marshmallow.

At the critical moment where we absolutely needed to get over, I quickly pulled ahead of a fast approaching bright red Honda Civic. In my rearview mirror I could see him shaking a fist at me, appalled at the added six seconds it would take to get him to his destination. Never-mind him though. Pedal to the metal and we're cruising now. Unhindered by the madness of the interior highways we made good time getting to the campground. It was crowded and full of ancient travelers in mega RVs, dwarfing our retired ambulance in both size and luxury. When we finally tucked into our spot, backing up so that our back doors could open out to the sea, it was almost two o'clock in the afternoon.

A deep sigh came from Sara and looking over she had unbuckled and splayed out all her limbs like a wilted starfish in her seat.

"I am so done with driving today. If we go anywhere we take a cab. I don't even care." She says while staring at the ceiling, her perfect dark curls splayed out over the top of her seat. I let out an agreeable laugh and unbuckle to head to the back of the van. Crawling over the bed and reaching to open the doors and a sudden whiff of perfect, heady sea air cleanses the cabin of the van. I open up a cupboard to find our stash and papers.

"I think I'll skin one up. Just the trick after that adventure." I say dully. She immediately pops up from her slouch and crawls back to join me on the bed. We sit together with our legs almost dangling outside the van. Our site was situated on a cliff, with the ocean nearly thirty feet below. The deep brownish red hue of the earth against the blue horizon added a new element. Sitting there and staring out to sea while doing my best to roll a joint was exactly the break that I needed. The pungent green nugs rolled into a semi decent joint and then lit without hesitation. It was time to push all of the early morning stress straight out to sea.

The waves were barely rideable now. Blown out and too fast. A winter storm was brewing somewhere far offshore and the sky had turned a steel gray and the forecast had called for a short spell of afternoon rain. The first tiny drops were starting to sprinkle our legs and feet so we shut the doors and laid back to take in the delicious sound of raindrops on a steel roof.

"You know what I could really go for?" I ask, completely stoned.

"Tacos?" She replies.

"Yes. Fish tacos. There's a place not far from here."

"God, that sounds amazing. And maybe a cold Pacifico with a lime?"

"Let's wait out the storm and then we can walk there along the beach." I say stretching out further and letting the weed permeate. That beautiful feeling of abandon that really only lasts for a few minutes before you're numb and dumb. The rain is streaking down our windows now and the sound is almost drowning out the waves as the peak of the storm roams overhead. The van is full of blueish smoke as the joint runs down to a nub and we smash it out in the built in ashtray at the side of the bed. Minutes go by and then an hour and then one more hour and the rain stops completely. Waiting for tacos can make one's mind wander into dark places.

"Alright. Let's blow this popsicle stand and get some tacos." I say, ready to stretch my legs and get out of the tin can van for even a few hours. Opening the doors and we are met with that gorgeous fresh smell of the rain and the sea. It's a clean smell, like a newborn baby or the first days of spring after a long winter. The air brings fresh vitality to our drug addled minds. The cobwebs start to clear and we clamber down to the beach. After the rain there are surfers already racing to grab waves. San Diego has a hefty population of over a million people. And sometimes it feels like they all surf. I hate that. I don't like to fight for waves. In a crowded lineup you can't tell what the vibe will be. Sometimes it's the best feeling in the world, but most of the time it's just full of assholes. Especially in bigger cities.

It's nice to walk on the hard sand after a rainfall. It can get tiring to wade through the soft earth. The walk is fairly straight and for almost the entire journey the tall cliffs on our left block out civilization and all that's left is the ever expanding horizon over the sea. It doesn't take long to get to the town of Encinitas and then finally up to the city taco stand. The vibe of the area is relaxed beach bum chic. Some of the richest ragamuffins you will ever meet live there. The stand is basically a small restaurant with a simple menu and outdoor seating but the quality of the food is memorable. A large salsa bar packed with fresh ingredients gives off a gorgeous scent from the long queue that we were standing in. After a few anxious moments in line we arrive at the front counter.

"Four al pastor and four carnitas por favor." I say in my best Spanglish. Moments later we have a tray of eight gorgeous, perfect tacos. The al pastor, marinated and carved from a roasted spigot of meat. Topped with fresh salsa and pineapple. If I was on death row, this would be my last meal. The carnitas are crisp after stewing all night and then tossed on a griddle. What's really special about Mexican tacos is the simplicity of the food itself. There's almost nothing to it. The most important part of the taco is arguably the tortilla. Is it fresh? Was it heated up on the grill long enough to allow for elasticity? If the quality of the tortilla is lacking they can fall apart or add a chalky texture that will set the dish off. Not this place. The tortillas are fresh and the ingredients lovingly prepared. It's only a few minutes later and we've finished off the tacos and were ready for more. "Let's do some fish tacos now. And a beer." She says after patting her belly like a sea otter and leaning forward in her seat.

Another round of tacos arrives at our table and this time it's four grilled fish tacos and four Baja fish tacos. There is an important distinction. The king of tacos in San Diego is the Baja fish taco. It has no equal. The fish is battered and fried in chunks or strips. Next add a coleslaw of fresh cabbage and then drizzle it with a lime crema. Good luck ever tasting something as pure and delicious. Grilled fish tacos are in their own element and don't count. They are the healthy option.

Fresh fish, sometimes swordfish or Mahi Mahi and a simple coleslaw. Each bite makes you feel like you should be a yoga instructor who runs ultra marathons for fun. Delicious but not nearly as satisfying as the cheaper, Baja fish tacos. The ice cold Pacificos with a lime wedge stuffed in the top are the perfect accompaniment. We have very few words between us in this twenty five minute experience. A hard, semi stoned focus permeates.

"Oh my god, that is delicious." She says with a mouth half full of fish taco. Washing the bite down with a sip of beer and a look of pure joy flushes her face. We clink glasses and just take in the freshness of the early evening. The sun has started its early descent and the rest of the night is ours to do with as we will.

"I say we hit up a bar before the walk back."

"Good idea."

Moments later we empty our tray in the bin and make a b-line for the bar across the street. It's a typical beach bar with your typical millionaire beach bum crowd. Where do people like this even come from? Some dark corner of a cookie cutter cul-de-sac. The scattered group of six or seven perfect specimens are lounged out by the short bar with a palm thatched roof. The men are deeply tanned with backwards hats and spotless board shorts that have never seen a wave. Strategically placed dark sunglasses straddle the bill of their hats and their million dollar smiles hide their shark teeth. The women are all replicas of the perfect Barbie doll suburbanite debutante whose jackal eyes scan Sara and I as we walk through the door. In short, it doesn't look like we'll be making any friends here.

The bartender is a friendly hispanic with a pep in his step and we quickly order two Mai Tais and lean up against the end of the bar. The conversation of the closest group of horribles is loud and centered around the disbelief that "Debbie" wore that dress to Tim's birthday party. Imagine if your life was built around the petty drama of the worst type of human, the American suburbanite.

Sara and I exchange quiet glances and sip on our fruity cocktail as nonchalantly as we can. The last thing we need is to upset the local wildlife. Our high from earlier in the afternoon is fading fast and we're still reveling in our satisfied stomachs after that perfect taco encounter. A moment later a hush runs through the group as a beautiful girl in a simple skirt and tank top enters the bar. It's Debbie and the tone has now completely shifted. Each of the girls shrieks in false pleasure and embraces her. They were like, so excited to like, see her. And oh my goodness doesn't she just look amazing. The look on her face is priceless. Out of the entire group she looks like she's the most down to earth. Less fake additions. A natural beauty that unfortunately for her friends requires little to no effort. She moves to the end of the bar near us and quickly gives us a smile before ordering a beer. Her friends have resumed a huddled conversation, this time about a different absent companion. She looks over at us and with a face that needs rescuing asks,

"Hello, how are you guys tonight?" In a voice that said, please rescue me from these horrible people.

"We're doing great. Just got to San Diego. Came over here after tacos across the street." I say with a smirk.

"Oh I love that place. Great food." She says, her voice already getting bored and drifting. She glances away at the door longingly.

"So, you have some interesting friends there." I say in a sarcastic tone. Both Sara and this new friend let out a laugh.

"Those are definitely not my friends. We all work at an office up the street. It's a mandatory social hour that my boss seems to like torturing me with." She says in a whisper. "Oh that sounds terrible, I don't think I would like that at all." Says Sara in a hushed tone with a smile on her face. "I'm Debbie." She says, raising her beer. "James and Sara" I say, while we all clink glasses and try to drone out the screeches and banter of the gaggle of geese next to us. "So where are you guys from?" She asks after taking a long sip.

"I'm actually from Poway but we've come from New York. On a road trip to Mexico." I say.

"Oh that's cool. Where in Mexico?" She asks.

"We don't really know yet. We know we want to make it down to La Paz but don't have any real plan." I say.

"My husband and I used to spend a lot of time in Cabo." She says dreamily.

"So what's it like at your job? I bet life is pretty good here?" I ask casually. Sara gives me a quick scowl of disapproval as if to say no, don't even think about it.

"Uh, well, it's pretty awful actually. I work fifty hours a week in a high stress environment where everything is demanded of me. I have a mortgage I can barely afford. I rarely see my husband or family and I have to put up with those sea monsters day in and day out. So yeah. It's kind of shitty." She says in a half joking tone but you can tell it cuts deep.

"Looks like the boss is here, nice talking to you guys. Enjoy Mexico." She says tiredly as she rejoins the sea monsters and a man whose cologne is probably more expensive than our van. Finishing our Mai Tais we tip the bartender and get up to leave. Just as we get to the door we look back at the group of plastic wealth and see our friend staring out the window, maybe dreaming of the old days in Cabo.

* * *

The sound of an RV leaving early in the morning woke us from our peaceful slumber. Today was going to be all about retracing my youth and Poway was the only way to start the day. Jumping back on the freeway, but this time early enough that the traffic was just starting to build. Considering the last few days of driving this was going to be a piece of cake to make it to my hometown and when we finally exited onto

Poway road my excitement was starting to grow. I had not been home in almost ten years and already I was noticing the changes. Lots of new development in the hills I had once explored. New shops and restaurants and traffic lined up on the other side of the road as early morning commuters headed towards the freeway.

"So this is Poway, the famous Poway." Sara says drolly. I can't blame her. So far there's nothing to really see. I point out the hills on our right as the place that my best friend had moved to after leaving the old neighborhood and then over there is where an infamous coffee shop had led to me asking out my first real girlfriend. Next door was sticks pool hall where rich kids liked to pretend they were tough and where I got my ass handed to me for the first time. There would be many more times. Just a little bit further up the road and we're passing the bowling alley and my first movie theater. Memories are flooding back as we drive past all of those places and memories that exist in the small places in your brain.

"I think I'll drive past the old house up on Buckskin trail. Then let's grab a breakfast burrito at Albertos." I say, turning right down Pomerado road towards the hills and my first real home. The many hundreds of days spent racing my friend on our way to school and home again. A horrible, violent memory of me witnessing a classmate get his leg run over by a semi truck as he was trying to cross the road. His screams still haunt me. I remember freezing in place and feeling like a coward for not racing to help him. I just stood there with my mouth open, staring.

Where there was once a massive field and a creek, now a sprawling cookie cutter neighborhood. Right there, on the corner of the lot is where I threw a dirt clod in my little brother's face. I was grounded for a week for that one. Turning left onto Metate lane and a second right onto Buckskin trail and there she was. The old homestead. The lawn had been turned into concrete and the tree where my dad had put together a small club house in the branches had been cut down. It's always jarring to see something ancient and sacred be altered in any way. It pulls you farther away from the memory until it's just a whiff of imagination. How many anxious hours did I spend in that tree house? How many heartbreaks did I suffer through in my room that looked out on the terraced backyard.

"Let's park up here at the dead end and I'll show you the creek where Jake and I used to have all kinds of adventures." I say while pulling over and putting the van in park. "Like the time you sat on skateboards and explored the sewer system?" She says with a joking grin.

"Hey, you don't know all of my stories. I didn't tell you about the time I tripped and fell into the cactus and…"

"And a piece of the cactus lodged in your knee." She says finishing my sentence. We both have a laugh and walk to the edge of the creek and look into the small stream of water that when I was little seemed like a river. All of those special memories of catching crawdads and racing paper boats after a big storm. Looking back at all of the magic it's a wonder we never noticed that it was really just a drainage from the hills and nothing more exciting than that. For us though it was an entire kingdom of imagination. The hours we spent gold panning and exploring every inch from the culvert to the place where it met the slope of the hill. I remember one adventure where a local mean kid was picking on my brother so I pushed him into the creek and then threw his bike after him. I got grounded for that one too.

The ancient memories were becoming too much to bare now and I made a motion to walk back to the van. There's an old saying that you never go home the same way twice and I believe that. Seeing the old house brought a mixture of emotions. A lot of difficult times took place in that mid century modern house with stucco walls and tiled roof. I still remember the day that my mother took me into the living room to tell me that my biological father had died from an overdose. My adopted father held me while weeping, telling me that it was going to be ok. I can remember how my tears soaked his sweater and he smelled of Polo cologne and cigarettes. The way my door made a clicking noise after I would slam it in protest to a punishment or in teenage angst. But I also remember all of the Christmas and Thanksgiving parties with happy relatives and warm smiles. There was still love here. But it was the hard kind of love that hits you in the face. Like an open palm or a rogue wave.

"Let's go get some food now. I think I've had enough of these memories." I say with a shaky voice. Sara reaches over and squeezes my hand and buckles her seat belt. There was so much to see but I didn't want to get sucked into the doldrums of memory. My stomach was growling and the only thing that was going to solve it was a bacon egg and cheese burrito from Albertos on Poway road. It had been there for as long as I can remember. A small adobe style Mexican joint with a small drive through that let out onto the street. Our van was too big to fit under the low hanging roof over the drive through so I jumped out and quickly ordered a breakfast burrito. You only need one for two people. It's the size of a small baby. Literally. Full of crispy bacon, scrambled eggs and cheese with refried beans and hash-browns. It being so early in the morning the world was just now starting to come out of their hiding places. We decided to stay in the parking lot to finish the burrito before hitting the road. Split in half it only takes mere minutes to finish leaving us both satisfied.

"Alright what's next to do on memory lane?" She asks after crumpling up the wrapper and tossing it in our small trash can strapped to the back of the seat. After rolling the window down to prevent the permanent burrito smell and inhaling a big gulp of fresh Poway air I immediately knew where to take her. "I think we'll go hike my favorite trail around Lake

Poway. Then maybe we'll drive by my old high school so I can add to the nostalgic pain." I say while pulling back onto the road.

"Sounds good. I can't wait to see where little Jimmy learned how to fish." She said coyly, knowing that it would be a story I would tell out loud in moments. Laughing I press play on the tape deck and soak in the familiar sites of Poway. The Irish bar and the country kitchen. The Honda dealership where I got my first car when I was seventeen.

"It's so weird being back on these roads. I spent so much time riding my bike up and down these back lanes." I say dreamily. Southern California in the late nineties was a special place to be. We stayed out late, riding our bikes anywhere we wanted to go. There was some crime, but it was usually minor. Just a nice little stretch of Americana and we were blessed to be a part of it for that short period of time. You never know you're in the good ol' days until they're gone.

"It kind of looks like upstate New York without the ghetto and the snow. Oh and you guys have more palm trees too." She says while peering out the window as we make our way towards the lake. Driving up towards Romona and then down again towards the valley so I can drive by the last house we lived in before I left for the Army and they moved to Cottonwood up north. You could just make out the drop off down the slope that led to our barn with the view over the valley. It was where I first started riding horses in the round pen in our backyard. Learning how to connect with a horse well enough to the point where it would let you ride it.

"Oh cool, look at that weird rock up on the top of the mountain." She says pointing up towards the range. "Oh yeah, that's Tooth Rock. We used to ride our horses up there all the time." I say casually. The massive boulder rests just on the top of some nameless mountain and resembles a pearly white. Get up close and it's covered in graffiti. So it goes. We continue past my favorite pizza place where my brother and I would sneak away to smoke weed behind the building and munch on slices of pepperoni the size of your arm. Then there was the Mexican restaurant with the good flautas and the ancient donut shop where the cool kids hung out at lunch.

Driving up past the high-school now. Poway High. The home of the Titans. It doesn't get more small town America than this right here. At the time it was the bane of my existence and seeing a few stray kids walking outside made me shudder to think of what they might be going through. "There's my high-school. Lots of memories there." I say with a nostalgic air.

"Oh yeah? Is that where little Jimmy got beat up everyday". She asks, laughing.

"No way, I was the king of the school." I say with a serious look on my face.

"Sure you were." She says drawing out her words and laughing hysterically.

"Alright, maybe I wasn't the king. But a few people knew my name." I say in a low tone.

"Yeah the janitor and a few teachers maybe." She laughs. "You're insufferable. I knew a few other people too." I say shyly.

We laugh and I realize that maybe the school isn't the best place to visit after all. The well maintained road continues on into the hills and up Espola road until a sign and a turn pointing the way to the lake. Driving past the water station and then into the verdant green grounds of the park. So many picnics and happy summer days were spent being let loose in the park. A long marina stretches out over the placid lake with the hills full of chicaree and oak trees. On the side of the lake an earthen dam holds it all in and provides all of that tasty and delicious drinking water. It's wild to think that this wasn't naturally a lake and that years ago it was just some random gulch. Man can occasionally get it right and I feel like Lake Poway is one of those good things.

Parking the marshmallow not far from the marina we begin our walk towards the oak covered hills. It's a strange thing coming home. Visiting all of those ancient places full of memories. Walking along the dirt path up past all of the fishing spots that get crowded on the weekend but now it's empty and it's like we have the whole lake to ourselves. The hike takes you around and up into the wilderness that separates Poway from the mountain town of Ramona. We wouldn't be going that far today. I just wanted to take her to an old spot that I once loved. And coming up on the left we had found it. An ancient oak tree with its roots exposed and hanging over a small cliff that hung over the lake. I used to love sitting amongst the gnarled tendrils, reading a book or maybe hiding from whatever reality I was running from that year. I wouldn't relive middle school for all the tea in China.

"This is my spot." I say, waving my hand in a big arc towards the lake. I wanted Sara to feel the warmth of the tree and to experience, even for a moment, the comfort I once took from its rough branches.

"It's nice." She says while touching the trunk of my tree. The look on her face is happy but unimpressed.

"You don't like it?"

"No I do, it's just that this is your tree. My tree is back in New York."

Walking away from my familiar place we continue along the waterfront and to a shady little hidden spot that my hooligan friends and I would come to when the park was too crowded. It was basically just two large boulders with a tree growing out from the middle of them. We stopped and leaned up against them to take a breather. The lake was starting to get a little choppy as the morning turned into the early afternoon and the sun climbed higher in the sky. Grabbing a few flat stones we did our best to skip them as far as we could and remained silent for over an hour. There were no words needed. We could just sit here and take in the moment. I think even Sara was impressed with the location. She was in her own little dream world of distant thoughts and long spent memories. For the last couple of weeks I had seen such bravery come from her. Months ago, in the busy office she had worked in, she had come close to a nervous breakdown. The stress of the corporate world had been weighing on her for years. Now, after everything we had been through she seemed lighter. Her proud chin was lifted high after quietly skipping the stone at least ten times. A smile that lit up her eyes but also held some semblance of sorrow. She was far away at her own little lake. But you could also tell that the future was far more important. The car breaking down had done something to her. She had shaken off her earthly shackles. She was ready to fly.

"I'm getting hungry again." She said quietly.

"I know just the place."

The walk back felt much shorter than the walk there and in moments we were cruising back through the small park and onto Espola road. "So, where to next, Captain?" She asks in an excited tone.

"I'm thinking we will go to Old Poway Park and eat at the world famous Hamburger Factory." I say with renewed enthusiasm.

"World famous huh? Like the whole world?" She says slyly.

"Well maybe just a tiny world. Great burgers and they serve a mean root beer float in a glass boot. It's high class stuff." I say as we once again cruise past the high-school of distant memories and only a little magic. It would only add to my confusion to stop here. Maybe in another ten years I'd revisit the place I had most wanted to run from. The drive was uninterrupted now. People were at work or in school and the clean city streets of my hometown sparkled with simplicity and innocence.

Old Poway Park is one of those historical spaces that probably never saw itself becoming a park where little kids' birthday parties would be perpetual. But it did. There is a working old world train that carries people a few hundred feet and a museum with lots of old western paraphernalia and of course the famous hamburger factory. When we were kids this was a treat that our parents would make us believe was of the highest order. We were lucky to even get a table, they said.

Everything seemed much smaller when we arrived. The wooden sidewalks that wrapped around the factory were new and not the same old worn boards that my brother and I had stomped on as kids. The girl who sat us was young and boppy. She probably went to Poway High and maybe even had the same teachers that I had struggled with. Maybe even the same dramas. Girl-loves-boy and boy-doesn't-love girl. Something like that. Maybe.

Inside the restaurant was almost exactly the same as it had been years ago. Old western regalia everywhere. Old saddles and rusty farm equipment hung up in various corners. A model train that in operation would make its way around the rim of the restaurant. Pictures of old west gunfighters and lawmen long forgotten by everyone but the Hamburger Factory. Our waitress approached and we were ready. Simple. Two cheeseburgers and two root-beer floats. Yes, we'll take some fries. Yes, have it all come out together. I wanted our last big meal in the US to be as American as possible and to be spread out before us like a great feast.

There's almost no one in the restaurant this being an afternoon on a school day and our food comes out quickly, in waves. First the fries, perfectly crisp and with an assortment of condiments. Then the burgers, whose circumference has not changed in twenty years. They are still the size of small dinner plates and you can smell the chargrilled meat sizzling between the sesame seed bun. Last, but certainly not least come the boot shaped root beer floats.

What happens in these next few moments can make or break your meal. What condiments do you put on the burger? Some will religiously say ketchup, mustard and mayo. Heavy on the ketchup. This is the wrong answer. Ketchup is a bastard condiment that should be banned from the burger. The only answer can be light mayo and a good amount of mustard. Ketchup should only be used for dipping fries into. This is an important process and if followed closely it will bring the best results. American food, as everyone knows, is just the imported ideas of starving immigrants from far away lands. But over the decades and centuries and eons we've managed to perfect it. The secret is in the sauce, as they say.

"This is a good burger." Sara says between ravenous mouthfuls.

"It's the best in the world." I say after taking a long sip of the root beer float to wash down the charred meat. You know the food is good when few words are exchanged and in less than twenty minutes we've settled back in our chairs with our hands on our bellies as full as ticks after the Fourth of July.

"Alright, that was pretty good." She says.

"It's the perfect last big meal before we head south." I say.

"So you're ready to do this?" She asks carefully.

"I'm as ready as I'll ever be." I say. She grabs a stray fry and nibbles on it. Her gaze hits me like a million degree laser beam over her spent root beer float as if to ask, are you sure?

"After visiting the ol' country, it just feels like it would be a mistake to go backwards. We've already started the adventure. The only thing to do now is to finish it." I say.

"Wasn't it an old Taoist monk that wrote that poem about an unbending tree? *An unbending tree will break in the wind.* Something like that." I say while standing to leave.

"Let's go be unbending trees then."

"Anchors away."

Walking out into the fresh afternoon air after a big meal and a vision for the future we were ready for the next step. Getting back into our marshmallow home and feeling the cozy lining of the seats. The smell of old car and woodsmoke soaked into the interior. We were ready. Ready to face the great unknown. Driving back towards our campground is a memory I no longer hold. I just remember that full, satisfied feeling before a big trip. The confidence and unfettered knowledge that our future may not be written but that we still had the pen with all of the words.

Chapter 16

The End of All Things

The border at San Ysidro is a hellish place. Arriving as early as possible made absolutely no difference. The cue seemed to stretch for a hundred miles and crawled by at a snail's pace. Inching closer and closer to the check point where a disgruntled border guard waves us through to the man with the gun who will take our passports. We put on our best cheshire grin and answer no to all of the questions. Do we have any guns? No. Do we have any drugs? No. Why are we coming to Mexico? To go surfing is my quick answer. The Mexican border guard then waves us on into Tijuana with a flourish of his hand. And just like that, we were in a completely different country.

Because it's still so early the lane begins to clear out as we ignore the off ramp for downtown Tijuana. We won't be spending any time in that area of despair. I had gone many times as a kid and it was always the same. Terrible crime and poverty masked over for the gringos out on a half day booze cruise. I had no use for the trinkets and cheap knock off watches that are sold in the markets. Or the photo opportunities to stand next to an abused donkey painted like a zebra. I'd leave that to the other pasty faced Americans with savage appetites and bellies that can never be filled.

Our first stop before taking on the deeper regions of the state was to be Ensenada. So, taking the coastal highway exit and passing through the apocalyptic outskirts of Tijuana was our only way forward. Driving at highway speeds and there not being much traffic helped speed us along but you could still see the dilapidated, squat, colorless homes crammed together against the border. The stark difference between the wealth and stability of San Diego, just a few miles north was shocking. The homes that sat right on the border with windows that gazed longingly north depressed me and I tried not to look but could not help it. It was like trying not to look at the car wreck on the side of the highway as you pass. This was Sara's first time out of the country and her head resembled a wind vane on a blustery day turning her neck from side to side, taking in the drama of the scene. Litter sprinkled the highway like confetti. The confetti of decades of corruption, neglect and poverty. What seemed like an hour passed as we navigated the light traffic heading south. Eventually the highway reaches the ocean and it begins to be a touch more touristy. Less of the overcrowded look and more of the cheap beach hotel and raucous bar scene. Every mile along the road to Rosarito has a sign advertising and catering to the wealthy gringo. A condominium complex being built would offer the finest in luxury accommodation along with award winning restaurants that had yet to be built. Rancho Esta las petunias. Or some such nonsense. Designed specifically for the suburban getaway to foreign lands. This was an excuse to not expand deeper into the culturally rich regions of the south. A trip of convenience considering the proximity to the border. I feel like it's a shame to jump into the water but only skim the surface. Mexico is a paradise of culture. You just need to get out of the border towns to find it.

Pulling in for gas at a colorful station just outside of Rosarito would be our only stop in this town. Petrol was cheaper here than it would be in the middle of nowhere. Placing the gas nozzle into the car tank and filling our marshmallow up to the brim in the best unleaded gas this side of the Rio Grande and all of a sudden two large SUVs from California pull up to the pumps on either side of us. In seconds a dozen people pile out of the vehicles, kids of all ages screaming and laughing and tugging at each other's hair with stressed out parents chasing after them. Locals standing outside the station shake their heads in disbelief as the kids run uncontrolled into the store. The parents fill up their suburbans, all packed to the gills with beach gear and enough luggage to last a year even though it's just for the weekend. Their loud accents cut through the quiet of the morning and in moments the whole gaggle of children are running back to the cars screaming even louder.

We look at each other and quietly move to jump back into our vans when one of the fathers in the suburban next to us notices our California plates.

"Hey man, where are you guys from? We're from LA. You guys headed to Rosarito?" He says in a friendly tone while putting the cap back on his gas tank.

" I'm from San Diego. No were headed further south. Trying to get away from the crowds." I say quickly, hoping to end the conversation before it can take off into introductions. At this point his wife and three of the five kids in his vehicle gather around to listen to our conversation.

"Honey, these guys are from San Diego. They want to go further south." He says with a half smile as if he knows something we don't.

"Oh don't do that. It's dangerous. Too many Mexicans for our taste. We like Rosartio." She says loudly so that the locals leaning against the shop can hear.

"Oh, have you been further south?" I ask hesitantly. I already know the answer but I want to hear her say it out-loud.

"No, I just know it's dangerous." She says with pouty lips. And then her kids are dragging her back to the car, screaming and fighting the whole way. The husband takes another look at us and gives us a little wave. The wave is insecure as if he's afraid of us. Afraid of the unknown and better to not talk to these strange travelers willing to risk the uncharted territories of the south. I'm left with an urgency to get as far away from people like this as we can. The brash, rude behavior of the gringo tourist is shocking to behold. They all pile back in their expensive Suburbans and race back up the road towards Rosarito and whatever hellish resort they're staying in.

"Wow. I do not want to be like that lady. And those kids are awful. Definitely does not make me want to be a parent anytime soon." She says after we clamber back into our home on wheels. We laugh as we continue past Rosarito on the open road. Now that we've left behind the majority of the tourist traffic it's all just locals and explorers on the road. The coastal road from Rosarito to Ensenada is beautiful at this time of year. The air is warm and you can smell the sea that stretches out on your right hand side as you head south. For the hour drive towards Ensenada the coast is just a stone's throw away and full of small resorts and then long stretches of inaccessible rocky beaches. It's not long before traffic starts to tick up a bit as we approach the medium sized city. Lots of trucks towing fishing boats full of Californians venturing as far south as most of them will make it.

"I don't really want to stop here do you?" I ask as we approach the city limits and see all of the color and craziness of the tourist town.

"No it doesn't look that nice but we also need to change our American dollars to pesos and maybe stock up on snacks." She says pointing to a colorful market and currency exchange. We pull off the road and get out, locking the doors carefully. The local scene is a little rough looking. Half old western and half post apocalyptic doom town. A stray dog with ragged, pointy ears sniffs our front tire and lifts his leg to pee. We dip inside and I head to the currency exchange booth while Sara grabs some vegetables and snacks to last a few days. Who knows what Santo Tomas will even have available. The lady behind the counter is short and squat. Fat and sturdy with jet black hair and native features, she looks at me with intelligent and scrutinizing eyes.

"Can I change this American money please." I say in an even tone, handing her a few hundred dollars.

Without saying a word she grabs the money and counts it quickly. Three hundred dollar bills. Slipping the cash under the till and counting out a few thousand pesos and handing me back a massive wad of sweaty currency felt silly. Like I was holding monopoly money. Three bills for a six inch stack. What a world. She doesn't look like she's in the mood to chat with this gringo so I just smile and thank her and find Sara.

Sara always thinks that she'll only be grabbing a few snacks and that getting a basket is a waste of time. It always ends up with her balancing a small horde of food against her breast and in between her fingers. A bag of chips balanced under her chin as she walks up to the counter and piles all of our goods on the table. Snacks, vegetables, a slab of skirt steak, some tortillas and a few fresh jalapeños. A six pack of ice cold Pacifico. How she carries all of that in her short arms is a mystery. Soon I'm peeling a few hundred peso off my stack and paying the disinterested check out lady. Back outside and into our giant, safe, marshmallow and were cruising back down Highway 1. This time the road takes a left inland, leaving the ocean behind. We're in the desert now. The hills alongside the highway remind me of Spain with sunbaked stones and scorched scrub brush. There's a peacefulness to the desert. At first glance it seems to be a dead place, but under its rough exterior lies a land teeming with life.

Once again I'm lost in a bygone world of Spanish conquistadors and fat friars, waddling up the coast of this barren land. Stopping where they could find water and food. Sometimes to satiation and sometimes to starvation. Each step forward for the glory of distant rich men. I like to think that a few of them were there for the experience. Life was pretty terrible in the 18th century for most of humankind. Why not have an adventure while you die of scurvy. The great unknown lasted a long time in the course of human history. It's only now in our digital age that satellites and the world wide web have saturated all of the corners of the world. But just for a minute imagine taking a very long walk into a completely unknown world with antiquated technology. These guys were moving by the stars. Portable compasses were just starting to be a thing. They had mastered the art of war but barely knew that eating a vegetable was essential to your health or your teeth fell out. The human body is weird.

* * *

The small village of Santo Tomas lies just south of Ensenada on highway one. It is a nowhere stop along the dusty highway surrounded by tall mountains that separate the sea and the desert. Our marshmallow home has performed wonderfully these last couple hundred miles. Ensenada and all of the adventures that took place there already seemed far away as we got out of the van for a snack and directions to the beach.

The taqueria is built in the classic adobe style and there are only a couple vehicles parked in the small lot. Next to the taqueria on an adjacent lot sits the ruin of an old church. All that remains is the wall that held the iconic triple bell tower. Like the one further north in California. Its crumbling facade shows the evenly placed bricks in small patches. From even a few feet from the door of the taqueria I can hear the mariachi music blasting and the smell of BBQ and meat wafting out into the street and making the air smell as delicious as a block party when you were a kid.

Inside the dimly lit restaurant are two caballeros in full regalia. Shining cowboy boots and riding chaps lead up to a colorful vest and ten gallon hat shaped sharply like the chicory that covered the hills. A colorful menu, lit up by bright lights is highlighted above the till and a bored but beautiful girl with jet black hair and an Indian nose waits for our order. To make it quick I scan the menu and just ask for a half dozen carne asada tacos and a couple Pacificos. She nods and accepts the pesos I had changed in Ensenada and shouts back to the kitchen our order.

"¿Dónde está Puerto Santo Tomas?" I speak in terrible Spanish. The girl looks at me and then clears her throat to respond, " I speak English." Her English is so perfect I almost want to press her as to why but the look on her face tells me to skip to the point. "We're trying to find the beach to camp at Puerto Santo Tomas." I say slowly. She shrugs and points outside to a small road that turns west into the mountains. "You follow that dirt road all the way to the coast, it will take you a couple hours." She says dryly. Moments later the chef who is sweating through his shirt brings a plastic bag wrapped tightly and hands it to me.

"Tacos" He says.

"Gracias amigo." I say in response with a big gringo smile and a thumbs up. He gives me a half smile that shows two gold teeth and then turns to go back to the kitchen. Walking back to the van I can see Sara, studying the map in the front seat, looking up as she smiles through the bug splattered windscreen at the treasures I carry.

"Oo la la. That smells amazing." She says as I hand her the bag of tacos.

"I'm going to fill up on gas here again. The lady said to take a right down that road and it's two hours to the beach down a dirt track. Should be an adventure." I say as she hands me one of the tacos from the bag. Stuffing it in my face in two bites because it's so delicious and fresh that I could eat fifteen more. I unscrew the gas cap and place the gas pump in and start to feel up the van when the girl who speaks English comes out to light a cigarette. She walks closer to our van and inspects it from afar. I give her a little wave and she acknowledges me with her eyes. "Do you know anything about that old church over there?" I ask her.

"It's the old mission. Very old. They used to grow wine behind it in the fields." She says distantly. Her gaze is far off now and looking towards the dirt road and the field behind the crumbling mission.

"When you go to the playa ask the fisherman for lobster. They will sell it to you there fresh, for a good price." She says again. This time it feels like she's offering a modicum of friendship after seeing my interest in the mission. She nods one more time and flicks the cigarette out onto the highway and disappears back into the taqueria.

"She said the fisherman will sell us lobster for a good price." I say after climbing back into the van and starting the engine.

"I'm ok with that." She says laughing.

Taking the right down the dirt road, our marshmallow home rumbles down the track leaving a trail of dust in our wake. The road carves its way through the coastal mountain range past a few ranches with the cattle meandering along the road. Taking the dirt track slowly so that we don't pop a tire or plow into a stray cow we notice a few smaller roads that peel off into the mountains. Not a human in sight. Just the cows, the red earth and the dust. The steep slope of the mountains are covered in the same chicory and scrub bush that we saw in southern California and it strikes me as remarkable how similar both places are. Nature doesn't change its dress for arbitrary borders.

Minutes turn into hours and the day is drawing to an end as we putter past the rickety old sign that reads, Puerto Santo Tomas, with an arrow pointing towards la playa and the campground. The old surfer was right, there's nothing here. A few scattered houses and a shack that from a distance looks like it could be a taqueria or bait shop or both. The campground as we approach is just a flat patch of grass that looks out over the half moon shaped bay. There is no one in the little shack that serves as the campgrounds headquarters. We are the only vehicle there as we pull into a spot that has a small BBQ pit and a picnic table. Backing up so that our bed looks out onto the sea and making sure the emergency brake is secure before we get out to stretch our cramped legs.

"Well, we're here. It's nice." I say

"It's perfect. Look at all of the boats in the bay." She says pointing to the left where an eroded cement ramp leads down into the sea. Scattered amongst the gentle waves of the bay are dozens of small fishing boats. But still no one. Not a soul to be seen. The only sound is the wind from offshore and the lapping of the small waves against the beach. A moment or two passes while we gaze out onto the sea, when out of nowhere a hunched over figure emerges from behind one of the sea shacks. It's an old man with ancient lines around his eyes and mouth and a slight limp to his gate.

"Bienvenida a puerto santo tomás. El precio es de veinte pesos por noche por favor." He says in a quiet voice.

"I think he said welcome to Santo Tomás and that it costs twenty pesos a night to stay." I say quickly to Sara while pulling my wallet from my jeans.

"¿Hablo Ingles?" I ask hesitantly. He smiles and says, " I speak a little."

"How long can we stay here?" I ask slowly, gesturing with my hand to the van and the site.

"Forever if you'd like." He says in a voice that drifts off to sea and floats out over the small boats and beyond to where the sun is just starting to slip beneath the horizon. I hand him some money and with a smile and a nod he quietly walks away without a word. There is something elvish about the old man. Something as old as the sea itself and in that moment we both feel the electricity of the old magic coursing through our veins. It begins at the top of the head and works its way into our bellies and all the way down to our toes.

"What do you think? Should we stay forever?" I ask while taking her into my arms and looking over at the golden sunset.

"I think I want to be here, in this moment, forever." She says, in her quiet voice with eyes glimmering softly in the light.

The water continues its gentle undulating movements and the boats rock back and forth as they have for centuries. In the distance the small houses are beginning to turn on their lights and the water is shimmering with their reflection. Time seems to stand still and for that brief moment a feeling of peace settles over us and all of the old world we had known disappears from memory. We had arrived. Along crooked roads of heartache and struggle to this tiny hamlet at the end of all things. All that is left is the magic and time and each other.

THE END

Epilogue

La Paz, Baja California Sur

The warm and dry wind rustled softly through the thatched rafters of the beach side gazebo. Sara is fast asleep next to me on a recliner with the sun bringing spiked shadows to dance on her face. The sound of the neon blue sea lapping against the shore had lulled her to sleep an hour before. The small, round table that separated us had two exotic, neon blue cocktails with a half eaten tower of fruit poking from the tops of the long tulip shaped glasses.

A few hours earlier we had just come from a car dealership where the man had handed us a wad of money for the keys to our marshmallow home. It was a hard parting. After nearly a year it was sad to say goodbye. She had sheltered us in all kinds of weather and kept the wolves at bay. But after enough time it felt right and we were ready for the next adventure.

I hated to wake her like this. She looked so peaceful lounging in the sun like a lizard. But it was time. We had been in La Paz for months now and the next step was calling. The winds of change were upon us and the electricity was starting to crackle and pop.

"Hey there sleepy head." I say quietly while stroking her hair. She began to stir slowly. A small smile and fluttering eyes open to reveal those perfect brown orbs of light.

"It's time to wake up. It's time to go to our new home." I say with a smile.

"Is it that time finally?" She asks, sitting up and leaning on her elbows in the recliner.

"It's that time. We meet the guy in just a few minutes on the pier for the title." I say, pointing to the long pier down the beach where our new sailboat bobbed gently in the quiet wake. With the early afternoon light playing against the rigging it almost looked like a spaceship that could carry us away into the cosmos.

"Did you get a postcard for Aldon and Sharon?" She asks as we walk towards the pier holding hands. The man with the title is standing next to our new home waving eagerly at us and we take one last look at land.

"Yep, I filled it out too. We can drop it off in the post box next to the pier." I say, handing her the card to look over. It's a glossy picture of the beach and just one simple line:

Dear Aldon and Sharon,
We found the magic!
With love, J + S

About the Author

Jason Bollinger is a UK based author with roots in America. When he's not traveling recklessly through Europe and the US he likes to spend his time with his daughter and wife eating pasta and listening to 1950s Italian pop and obscure country music. This is his first novel.

Printed in Great Britain
by Amazon